SEALED WITH A KISS

A Star Lake Romance

LORANA HOOPES

Sealed with a Kiss
Copyright © 2020 by Lorana Hoopes
All rights reserved.

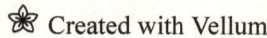 Created with Vellum

NOTE FROM THE AUTHOR

This book is dear to my heart. I've always loved the small town feel and the crazy characters that generally live there. I hope you enjoy the story and the characters as they are dear to my heart. If you do, please leave a review at your retailer. It really does make a difference because it lets people make an informed decision about books.

Below are all the books in the small town series. I would love for you to check them out. I'd also like to offer you a sample of my newest book. Free Sample!

Sign up for Lorana Hoopes's newsletter and get her book, The Billionaire's Impromptu Bet, as a welcome gift. Get Started Now!

The rest of the Star Lake series:
When Love Returns

Once Upon A Star

Love Conquers All

LORANA HOOPES

A Star Lake Romance 3

Love
Conquers All

❧ I ❧

MAX

Max pulled at his blue and red striped tie again. He hated ties. Hated the look of them with their perfect knots and pointy ends and hated the way they felt around his neck like they were cutting off his air supply. A sadist must have invented them, someone who liked feeling like they had a noose around his neck all the time. Someone who didn't know the comfort of a well-worn flannel shirt with the top two buttons undone and plenty of room for his neck to breathe.

He never wore ties or dress shirts even, and he couldn't believe he was wearing them today. Scratch that. He couldn't even believe he was here today. Sitting in an uncomfortable folding chair surrounded by people he didn't want to talk to. Even the hum of their muted conversations annoyed him. He'd rather be anywhere else, but

Layla was his friend and it would have been rude not to be here.

The problem was… It should be him at the front of the church. Not that he wanted to be wearing a silly monkey suit and flashing a fake smile at all the people in the congregation, but he wanted to be the one marrying Layla. He had since they were in high school, but he'd never gotten the courage to tell her.

Prom night had been the closest he'd come. Of course, she'd gone with Bruce Bollinger, captain of the basketball team - Star Lake was too small to even have a football team - but Bruce had left her in the middle of the dance floor to talk to some cheerleader from a neighboring town who had crashed their dance with a group of her friends. His heart had broken for her that night as he saw her freeze in the middle of the dance floor like a deer in headlights.

Max had swooped in and led her off to a secluded corner. He had offered his shoulder to cry on, and she'd accepted, soaking his jacket with her tears and filling his nose with the sweet scent of her shampoo. He wanted to tell her how he felt then, but it hadn't seemed right. Not with her heart so newly trampled.

So, instead, he'd held her until her tears stopped. Then he'd danced with her and joked with her and told himself he'd get the chance to tell her how he felt soon. He'd walked her home in the moonlight, trying to ignore the romantic setting and fighting the urge to kiss her as she stared at him under the soft porch light.

"Thank you, Max," she'd said as she inserted her key in the front door. "I appreciate you being there for me. I must be a terrible judge of character. It's a good thing I'm swearing off men." And then she'd entered the house and closed the door. He'd walked home that night wondering how he could convince her that he wasn't like the other men she'd dated but coming up with no answer.

A few months later, she'd begun seeing someone new, and after graduation, she'd decided she wanted to see the world. With him. Max's heart had broken for the second time.

He was comfortable in Star Lake. He'd been born here, and he was a homebody. He liked working in the diner his father had opened. He enjoyed the slower pace of small-town life. He had no desire to go and see the world. What he saw on television - though he rarely watched it - was enough for him, and so he'd said goodbye to the woman he loved without telling her.

He'd tried dating a few times after she left, but not only was the dating pool small in Star Lake, but Layla had ruined him. No other woman had her smile, her vivacious personality, her quirky nature. So, he'd given up on the thought of love. Then his mother had died, and his father, unable to bear the pain, had retired and left the diner to him. Max had pretended that was enough. And then Layla had come home. Alone.

They'd fallen right back into their old routine. She'd come over every morning for coffee, harass him about his flannel shirts and ball cap, beg him to put something new on the menu, and flash her crooked smile on the way out the door as she went to work. He'd been so glad to have her back that he hadn't thought there was any rush in telling her how he felt. And then Randall Jones had swooped in and whisked her off her feet. Now, here he was sitting in the stuffy church, wearing a scratchy shirt and a noose around his neck as he waited to watch the woman of his dreams get married to someone else. Suddenly, his life felt a little like an old Western. Or a sad country song.

"Do you think this wedding is even going to happen?" Ned leaned over the empty seat Max had purposefully tried to leave between them and invaded his personal space. The odd man had a way of rubbing on his last nerve though Max wasn't sure if it was his Alfalfa hair or his habit of asking incessant ridiculous questions. "You think she ran? Maybe we have our own Runaway Bride."

Max rolled his eyes as he glanced around for a clock. He never wore a watch, but thankfully the church had a small clock above the door. It was ten after two, but Layla was notoriously late to everything, so there probably wasn't any need to worry just yet.

"Some people really should learn to be on time,"

Barnard piped from his other side. His too-small jacket bulged against his belly, and though Max was sure he thought he was whispering, his voice still carried through the small room. Barnard was the mayor, and he loved nothing more than hearing his own voice, even though the sound was like nails on a chalkboard to Max. "Some of us have other things we could be doing."

Max doubted Barnard had anything interesting waiting for him at home. Besides himself, the man only showed an interest in stamps and chess. Nothing exactly riveting in Max's book, but then he was pretty sure most people thought the same of him.

"Maybe she took my advice," Paula chirped up from behind him. Max turned to see her lean toward him, her bright red dress stretching across her ample frame. No one, except for Paula who was always looking for attention, would wear red to a wedding. "I told her not to marry him. He's not from Star Lake."

Max furrowed his brow at her, wondering if she realized Layla wasn't originally from Star Lake either. However, she'd become such a part of the town that he often forgot she hadn't been born here as well.

As if she hadn't seen his look or didn't understand it, she continued. "Plus, there are certainly more handsome men here who would love to be with Layla." She shot him a pointed look as she said the last statement.

Did she know of his feelings? Had she told Layla? Was he

the reason she hadn't shown? Should he try to find her? He wrestled with his emotions and his tie a few moments longer before standing and edging out of the aisle. He felt the eyes on him as he made his way toward the back of the small church, but he refused to look back and give them any satisfaction.

There were only a few rooms outside of the small sanctuary. Besides the bathrooms, one was the pastor's office, one was used as the Sunday school room, and he had no idea what the other was used for, but he made his way in their direction.

Kitty, Layla's best friend, stood outside the Sunday school room. Her auburn hair was pulled back in her signature fifties' style making her appear put together, but her hands fidgeted with something white and a worried frown covered her face.

"Where's Layla?"

She turned wide eyes in his direction and bit her lip. "I don't know. She said she needed some air, but that was ten minutes ago."

"Okay, stay here. Do you have any idea where she might have gone?"

Kitty shook her head and clenched her hands tighter. "She always goes to the diner when she needs to get away, but she knew you were here."

He placed a hand on her arm to try and ease her anxiety. "I'll find her. Don't worry."

She nodded though she didn't look convinced, and he headed for the outside door. As he pushed it open, he lifted his hand to shield the sun. It shone brightly as if it had no idea the storm cloud brewing in the small church. He paused, thinking of where Layla might have gone. Back to the bed and breakfast she ran? Would she sit on his front step? And then it hit him.

In the middle of town, there was a huge weeping willow with branches that seemed to kiss the ground. He'd found her there years ago when her parents separated and she felt her world was falling apart. Knees pulled to her chest, she had been the picture of innocence and sadness. It would be the perfect place for her to go now, especially with most of the town inside the church.

Why had she run though? Was it just nerves or could it be that she realized Randall wasn't the guy for her? And if that was the case, did he have a chance? His heart did a funny little dance in his chest, and he pulled at his collar again, wishing he was wearing his comfortable flannel instead of this stiff dress shirt.

The tree came into view, the branches bending toward the ground as if pressed by some invisible force. Squinting, he thought he could make out a patch of white beneath the low branches. She was there, probably with her knees curled to her chest and grass stains on her backside, but then Layla had never been the type to care what people thought about her. That was just another thing he loved about her.

He spread the soft branches of the tree and crawled in next to her. His dress shirt pulled at his shoulders as he tried to get comfortable, and he loosened the tie from its death grip on his neck. She lifted her head and smiled at his awkwardness.

Leaning against the trunk of the tree, he cleared his throat. "You know, the wedding is supposed to be happening over there in the church." He pointed to his left, but offered her a crooked smile to soften his words.

"I know, but I couldn't go through with it."

His heart lifted at her admission, but he tried to play it cool. He was her friend first and foremost. "Why not? I know Randall doesn't have my skills in the kitchen, but he seems like a nice guy."

She sighed and leaned her head against the tree. Her hair was nearly the same color of the trunk except for the soft red highlights that ran through hers, and her head was close enough to his that he could once again smell the sweet scent of her shampoo. "He was nice, and I thought that was enough, but as I was getting dressed today, the thought of marrying him just made me feel…" She paused and bit her lip. "Bored. Is that awful? I'm so awful." Her head fell back to her knees.

Max placed a hand on her shoulder and fought the urge to pull her into his arms. "It's not awful. It's smart. Yes,

Randall might be hurt, but believe me, he'd rather know now than marry you and find out later."

She sniffed and lifted her eyes to his. He wanted more than anything to wipe her tears away and touch her lips with his, but it wasn't the right time. It seemed to never be the right time. "I don't know what's wrong with me. I don't even need to be married. Now that I'm running the bed and breakfast, I can take care of myself."

But Max knew. Yes, financially she could take care of herself, but Layla's parents had split when she was in high school and her father had run off with another woman and had more children. She rarely saw him after the divorce, and her self-esteem had taken a hit whether she knew it or not. So, while she could financially provide for herself, she was looking for someone to love her like her father hadn't, but he couldn't tell her that. Instead he'd have to show her that he was the man who could do that. The man who had been and would always be by her side. The man who would wipe her tears at night and bring her coffee in the morning. He just wasn't sure how.

"You know what?" she continued, "I know I've said it before, but this time I mean it. I'm swearing off men until I really know what I'm looking for. That's only fair, right?"

It was, and Max just hoped that it gave him time to show her that what she was looking for was right in front of her face.

❧ 2 ❧
LAYLA

Layla smiled as she took Max's hand and let him lead her out from the willow tree. He always seemed to be there when she needed him. He'd been there when her parents split, when her father remarried, and when her high school boyfriend dumped her at prom. She was so fortunate to have a friend like him.

"Do you think everyone is going to be mad?" She bit her lip as they made their way back toward the church. She certainly had made a mess of things, and she really needed to figure herself out before jumping into another relationship.

Max turned to her, his brown eyes full of compassion. "Are you kidding? Nobody cares about the wedding; they just want the free food. Since it's already made and paid for, just tell them the party is still on. I bet no one other than Randall will be upset at all."

Layla laughed, but she knew he was right. The best thing about small town life was the camaraderie, and Star Lake was not short on that. Nor were they short on quirky characters. There would probably be a few people who talked about the cancelled wedding for a few weeks, Paula included. That woman would gossip about anything she could get her hands on, but she was also fiercely loyal. Layla guessed it went with the territory and really if a few sideways glances and a little gossip was all she got from this; she could count herself lucky.

When they reached the church, Layla took a deep breath before pulling open the door. Kitty still stood outside of the office door where she'd left her, only now she was a nervous mess. Tiny white dots covered the floor at her feet, and Layla realized she had shredded a napkin to bits.

Her eyes widened when she caught sight of Layla, and she stalked over as fast as her short legs would allow. "Layla Montgomery, what do you think you were doing leaving me here? People have been asking me where you were and I didn't know what to tell them."

Layla bit her lip and offered an apologetic smile. "I'm sorry, Kitty. I just needed some air." She should have remembered how high-strung Kitty was and that leaving her without an explanation would send her into a tizzy.

Kitty had been her best friend since the eighth grade when she moved into town. Even then, she had dressed as if she lived in another decade. Most of the kids had found her weird, but Layla had found her refreshing. She was definitely different, and Layla liked that.

Kitty pushed her cat-eye glasses up with one perfectly manicured fingernail and sighed. "It's okay. I should have figured something was up when I was doing your hair. I've never seen you look so pale, but I thought it was just nerves."

Kitty was also the resident hairdresser and had been doing Layla's hair for years. It had only been natural that she would ask her to do her hair on the most important day of her life. Only it had turned out not to be the most important day of her life.

"I thought it was just nerves too," Layla said, "but as I sat under the willow tree, I realized it was more that."

Kitty's wide eyes looked from Layla to Max and back again. "So, there's not going to be a wedding?"

"No, but there is going to be a reception."

Kitty began fanning herself with her hand and leaned against the wall. "Oh dear, I don't think I'll be able to handle the stress. Do you mind if I stay here while you tell them? I can't deal with accusing eyes." She pointed weakly toward the sanctuary.

Layla chuckled and squeezed her friend's arm. "Don't worry. You can stay right here until I come back. I bet Max will even stay with you." She looked to Max who opened his mouth as if he wanted to protest but closed it when she mouthed the word "please" at him.

"Yeah, sure. I'll stay with you. It's not like I need to get the food ready or anything."

Kitty brightened. "I could help you with that. It would certainly take my mind off of the stress."

"Fine," Max grumbled, "but you do what I say. Not the other way around, got it?"

Layla bit her laughter back as she watched her two closest friends argue. She was definitely lucky. If only she could skip the next few minutes. Seeing the disappointment in Randall's eyes was not something she was looking forward to.

She paused at the sanctuary doors and took a deep breath. She could do this. As soon as she swung them open, the pianist began playing the wedding march. Layla cringed. She had been hoping to tell Randall first, but there was no way she was walking up the aisle to that.

"Sorry, can you please stop playing?"

Beula, the pianist, was an elderly woman. She was still a beautiful player but nearly deaf, and she seemed not to hear Layla's request as her fingers flew over the keys.

"Beula?" Layla hollered a little louder. Someone near Beula stood and tapped her on the shoulder.

The music stopped and Beula looked up in surprise. "What?"

"There's no need to play anymore, Beula. There isn't going to be a wedding." Layla glanced Randall's direction and then quickly away when she saw the hurt in his eyes.

"No wedding? Then what on earth did you gather us all together for?" Barnard asked, standing and tugging on his jacket.

"Yeah, I got dressed up in my Uncle Albert's suit," Ned added.

Layla held up her hands to stop the bickering. "There's still going to be a reception. Max is getting it ready now, so why don't you all head over to the bed and breakfast?"

The bickering turned into a hum of excitement as the crowd began spilling out of the sanctuary.

"You know, you didn't have to fake a wedding to have a party," Paula said as she marched out the door in her bright red dress.

Layla shook her head and continued up the aisle to Randall. This was the part she'd been dreading, but she figured it was like a band-aid. Best to rip it off as quickly as possible. "I'm sorry."

He shrugged. "I guess I kind of knew. You didn't seem that into planning the wedding which should have been my first clue. Can you at least tell me why?"

"You're a great guy, Randall, but I realized that I don't know what I'm looking for right now and marrying you wouldn't be fair. To either of us."

He nodded as if he understood though she doubted he

did. She didn't really understand herself. If she had, she never would have let it get this far. "Well, if you change your mind…"

"I won't," she said, interrupting him. The last thing she wanted to do was give him any more false hope.

"I see." His voice had taken on a nasally tone or maybe it had always been there. Regardless, Layla realized she didn't really like the sound of his voice, and she couldn't imagine listening to it for the rest of her life. "Well, if it's all the same to you, I think I'll skip the party."

"Right, of course." Layla leaned in to hug him, but he pulled back and she was left standing awkwardly with her arms raised. Slowly, she lowered them, feeling like a complete idiot. It was understandable that he didn't want her to touch him. "Well, I guess I'll see you around then." The words felt flat and stupid as they came out of her mouth. Here was a man she had almost married and she was acting like they had just gotten together for coffee instead of breaking his heart. Why did her mouth always have to react faster than her brain?

He nodded, shoved his hands in his pockets, and shuffled out of the side door of the church without another word. Layla felt awful for hurting Randall, but Max was right. It would have been much worse if she had waited until after they were married to realize he wasn't the man for her.

She waited a few extra minutes to make sure he would

be out of eyesight before she exited the church and headed to the bed and breakfast. The noise of conversation and music carried out to her before she even opened the door.

Paula stood just inside the small entryway, her large frame taking up the majority of space and causing Layla to squeeze against the wall to get around her. "I knew you would come to your senses," Paula said, laying a hand on her arm as she passed. "We all knew Randall Jones wasn't the right man for you." She emphasized the word *wasn't* as if she and everyone else knew who the right man was.

"Uh, thanks, I think." Layla wasn't sure what the right response was to something like that though she assumed Paula wanted her to ask who the right man was. She wasn't going to play into that game though. Nope, she'd decided no more men until she figured herself out a little more.

"So, now that the wedding is off, does that mean I can get the toaster back that I gave you?" Ned asked as he came up to her. "I could use it for my house. Mine blew up the other day for some unknown reason. Smoke filled the kitchen and I had to open the windows to keep the smoke detector from going off. Had them open for hours, but it still smells burned in there."

Gifts. Yes, she would have to give all the gifts back. It was too bad because she was certain someone had bought her the cappuccino maker she had placed on her wish list. That was a shame to lose.

"Of course she will return the gifts." Barnard's

pompous voice carried over the noise of the others. "It would be highly improper to keep them and while Layla has her faults, she is aware of proper etiquette."

Her brow furrowed as she wondered just what faults he was referring to. "Yes, I will make sure all the gifts are returned to the giver. It might just take me some time, but if you know what your gift looked like, you are welcome to take it with you when you leave."

That earned a cheer from the people in the immediate vicinity, and Layla took the opportunity to continue to the kitchen. She pushed open the swinging door and sighed as she leaned against it. At least it was quieter here.

"Everything okay?" Max asked as he looked up from the counter where he was assembling some beautiful dish.

She bit back a smile as she watched him. He was an anathema for sure. Rugged and surly on the outside but inside there was this other part of him. Refined and sweet. He could have probably left Star Lake and been a famous chef anywhere else, but he seemed attached to the town. All he'd ever talked about was taking over his dad's diner and adding his own flair to the place. He'd certainly done that, but she wondered if he ever wanted more.

"It's fine," she said, answering his question. "Just needed to get away from the crowd for a minute."

He snorted softly as he pushed the finished plate toward Kitty and began another. "Why do you think I like hiding out in the kitchen?"

She had always wondered, but she could understand now. Besides, he looked completely at home in the kitchen, even though it wasn't his normal one. She watched him work for a few minutes - she could really use some pointers from him. Maybe he could give her some as they worked on the upcoming festival together.

Every summer, Barnard planned some big festival to try and drum up business for the town. This year, he had planned a week-long Star Lake Days of Summer festival. Every business owner had teamed up to take on a day and showcase what they did best. Layla was glad she had been paired with Max though she still had no idea how best to showcase the bed and breakfast. It wasn't like she could wash laundry or answer phones as a demonstration which seemed to be how she spent most of her time nowadays.

Oh well, there would be time for that later, and maybe Kitty would have some ideas. That woman was a bundle of ideas, and, unlike Ned's, hers usually made sense.

"Layla, grab a few plates and help me get this food out there. You need to be socializing with your guests anyway, not hiding out here in the kitchen with Oscar the grouch," Kitty said as she placed three plates on a large serving platter.

"I'm not grouchy," Max said under his breath as Layla grabbed a plate. She bit back a smile as he huffed. He might not be grouchy underneath, but that was certainly the image most people had of him. It was too bad he didn't show other people the side she saw of him.

Pushing the thought out of her mind, she followed Kitty back out into the crowd. Okay, a crowd might be a slight exaggeration. There were probably fewer than thirty people in the dining room and living room, but people in Star Lake tended to have big personalities which made them feel like more than their actual number. She would certainly be glad when this party was over and she could rest her feet and relax.

It was four hours later when the last guest left. Nearly all of them had taken their gifts with them, leaving only a handful still on the coffee table in the living room that she would have to hunt down the owners of.

The door to the kitchen swung open and Max and Kitty stepped through. "The kitchen is all clean," Kitty said.

"Guys, you didn't have to do that." Layla felt badly that her friends had worked so hard for an unnecessary party.

Max shot Kitty a pointed look and folded his arms across his chest. "That's what I told her."

Kitty swatted his arm and shook her head. "The wedding may have been canceled, but we said we would take care of the food and that means cleaning up after it too."

Layla's throat tightened with emotion. She really did

have the best friends a girl could ask for. "Thank you both. For everything."

"Nonsense. That's what friends are for." Kitty gave her a tight squeeze. "I'll come check on you tomorrow."

Max shuffled his feet, appearing unsure if he should hug her as well, so she took the guesswork from him and wrapped her arms around him. "Thank you," she said again and waited for him to return the hug.

His arms circled her, and he tapped on her back lightly before pulling back. "Call me if you need anything or you just want to talk."

His words tightened the feeling in her throat. She was lucky, and yeah, she had acted stupidly rushing into the romance with Randall after getting her heart broken but there was no need to do that again. She had Kitty and Max and everything she needed right here in Star Lake. Romance could wait.

MAX

Max laid the menu down in front of Paula and tried his best to ignore her pointed stare. At nearly fifty, Paula thought she was wiser than everyone else - except possibly Barnard - and she was attempting to use that flawed logic with him now. Her and the rest of the town, it seemed.

It had been two weeks since Layla's cancelled wedding, and everyone who entered the diner appeared to either shoot him a look or drop a hint that now was the time to make his move. But it wasn't.

Layla needed time.

He didn't want to be the rebound guy, and besides, he'd heard her say she wasn't ready for another relationship. Telling her how he felt now would only earn him yet another heartbreak and turn their relationship awkward, and he didn't want that. Especially not with them having to work on the festival together.

"I don't mean to state the obvious," Ned began from his position a few feet away.

"Then don't." Max didn't even bother to watch Ned's jaw drop as he passed the counter and entered the kitchen. He loved the small-town feel, but he hated how everyone felt it was their right to butt into his business. He knew what he was doing. Well, that wasn't entirely true. He had no idea how long he might have to give Layla, but he was working on reading her cues.

She and Kitty came in every morning, and he had learned to discreetly watch them while he cleaned the counter or served up food. He'd picked up on a few cues, and he was sure that when Layla was open to the idea of love again, he would know it.

"Well, good morning, Layla." Paula's voice carried through the swinging kitchen door. She was normally a loud mouth anyway, but she had obviously upped her volume to give Max a heads up at Layla's arrival. He shook his head as he scrambled up the omelet Ned had ordered and folded it onto a plate. Carlos, his helper, was working on his own masterpiece at the oven next to him and bopping to the music playing in his ears.

Normally, Max would find it rude for an employee to listen to headphones at work, but cooking was a pretty solitary job anyway, and as long as Carlos got the orders out on time, he didn't mind if the man never spoke.

He placed the plate down in front of Ned and walked away before the man could make any other awkward comments that Layla might hear. Though he knew what she and Kitty would order, he grabbed menus from the end of the counter anyway and placed them down on the table in front of them.

Layla's dark hair was down today and flowed to her shoulders. He'd touched it once or twice over the years and knew that it was as soft as it appeared, and he forced his hands to stay by his side. Touching it now would certainly earn him creeper status.

"I'm going to assume it's the usual today," he said as he stood at the end of the table, hoping his nerves didn't show.

Layla looked up and smiled. "I don't know why you bring us menus, Max. We sit at the same table every day and order the same meals." It was true. She had staked claim to a table, and while Max would never shoo a customer out if they were to sit at her table, she had been known to wait until it cleared before sitting and ordering. Usually while tapping her fingers loudly on whatever surface was nearby and fixing a stare on the perpetrator. Of course, the regulars knew it was her table, but every once in a while, a visitor would pass through town, and as

Max's diner was one of the few places to eat, they would inevitably stop in to partake of his famous burgers.

"I guess I would hate to overstep and assume on the one day you decided to be different." He flashed his own smile back and scooped their menus up. "One order of chocolate chip pancakes with a side of bacon and one all-star breakfast coming right up."

Layla had been ordering chocolate chip pancakes and bacon along with a large cup of coffee for as long as she'd been coming into the diner. He'd thought she was kidding the first few times she ordered them because that wasn't a normal grown woman's order, but she'd been adamant. So, he'd made them, adding a smile and a hat like he did for the kids who ordered them, and she'd eaten every bite, proving his theory that she was still a kid at heart.

Kitty, on the other hand, ate the more grown-up breakfast. Two eggs, two slices of bacon, and two pieces of toast - always sourdough and always eggs over easy. He could see why the two of them got along so well, at least in the area of consistency. After scribbling the order down on the pad, he placed them on the silver spinner and dinged the bell until Carlos nodded that he'd seen them. Max would decorate Layla's pancakes, but allowing Carlos to make them gave him the opportunity to stay where he could see and hear Layla better.

He fished out two porcelain mugs from under the counter and filled one with tea and the other with coffee, black but with two pumps of caramel and a splash of hot fudge. Then he returned to Layla and Kitty's table and placed the mugs down.

"What do you think, Max?"

Layla was looking at him with those soul-sucking eyes, and he realized she had asked a previous question he had not heard the answer to. "I'm sorry, I must have missed the beginning. What do I think about what?"

"Hosting our day at the bed and breakfast."

Their day? Had he missed something? And then it hit him. The stupid festival day that Barnard had arranged. He was supposed to host that day with Layla. He would display his cooking - which would of course cost him financially here at the diner, but Barnard didn't seem to think about that - and she would display... How on earth was she supposed to display the bed and breakfast?

"I was asking if you would be opposed to hosting the day at the bed and breakfast instead of in the town center? I can't think of any other way to advertise the bed and breakfast. Plus, it would give you access to the kitchen." She smiled up at him, a hopeful expression on her face.

She needn't have bothered trying to butter him up. His mind was already spinning with how much time this would give them together. "I think that's actually a great idea." He might just have to thank Bernard after all. "I could have Carlos cover a few of the customers here and send the others to the bed and breakfast. That way they have a comfortable place to eat and I don't lose all my business."

Her smile widened, sending his heart into that funny skipping dance again. "You could never lose all your business. Other than my place for breakfast, there's no real place for anyone to eat in this town."

"I don't know. Someone just bought the old laundromat across the street. What if they turn it into a restaurant?"

"What?" She bolted from her seat and hurried to the large glass window. "How did I not know about this?"

Layla was generally one of the first people in town to be "in the know", but he knew her head had been focused on her wedding and then the repercussions of the cancellation of it the last few months. "You were a little busy," he said, shuffling his feet.

Shaking her head, she returned to her seat. "Crazy. That's what I was. It's definitely a good thing I swore off men."

She didn't notice the heads that shot up at her statement like groundhogs popping out of holes, but Max did. Maybe now Paula and Ned would leave him alone about telling Layla how he felt. It was clearly not the right time.

The bell from the kitchen dinged, alerting him that Layla's and Kitty's food was ready. Relief flooded Max as he entered the kitchen and grabbed the plates. He added his usual flair plus a little something extra to Layla's pancakes and then returned to their table.

Layla laughed as she spied the clown hat and bow tie Max had added to the plate. "Max, you are too fun. You really do spoil me."

Coughs erupted from Ned, and Max glared at him. "You might want to get something for that cough, Ned." He emphasized the man's name and hoped he understood the implied meaning.

"We should probably get together soon and work out the menu and a schedule," Layla continued as if she didn't hear the commotion going on a few feet away.

"I'm free tonight after closing." Max mentally kicked himself at the eagerness of his words. They had flown out of his mouth without him thinking about it.

Her lips pursed for a minute and then broke into a smile. "I can make tonight work. See you at eight?"

He couldn't wait.

❦ 4 ❦

LAYLA

The sun was just setting as Layla approached the diner that evening. Max always stayed open until eight, but he rarely had customers after seven. The people of Star Lake liked to hole up in their houses by seven thirty and watch game shows or play card games. Actually, she wasn't sure what most of them did in their houses, but that was how she imagined them.

A bell announced her arrival with a bright tinkling sound as she pulled open the door, and Max looked up from the counter he was wiping down. His lips broke into a wide smile, and for a moment, she saw the boy she remembered from high school. He'd been different then, still reserved and yet opinionated, but not the short, sarcastic man he had developed into. She wondered when that change had happened. Probably when she'd been gone from Star Lake. Perhaps that time had been as disastrous for him as it had for her.

"Grab a seat," he said, pointing to her favorite table. "I had some time today, so I wrote down some menu ideas."

"Good because I was too busy today to do much of anything besides answer the phone and put out fires." She collapsed into her favorite seat and sighed.

"Busy is good though, right?" He rummaged behind the counter for a bit and then produced a yellow legal pad and a pencil.

"Yeah, it is, but I'm going to have to look at getting some more help. Emma is no longer cutting it." She'd only recently bought the bed and breakfast, and it had been in the red when she'd signed the papers. Starting new with just herself and one part-time person had seemed to be the best way to start turning a profit at the time. She'd just had no idea how much work was involved.

Max sighed as he sat down beside her. "Taking over and changing things is never easy, but I think it's worth it in the end."

She knew he was talking about the diner. His father had definitely run it differently, and Layla knew Max had taken some flak for the changes when he first took over. "How is your dad?" It was the first either of them had spoken about him since Max's mother passed and his father up and left Star's Lake.

Max's jaw clenched, and his posture stiffened slightly. "He's okay, I guess. Haven't seen him in a few months."

Layla wished she had words to comfort him, but she was unsure what the best words would be. He and his father had been on rocky ground before his father left, and after... well, that had been when she was gone. When she'd returned, Max had changed. Plus, her relationship with her own father was disastrous. She was certainly not one to be doling out advice in that department. Still, she felt the need to say something. "Do you remember the time you recommended a Hawaiian burger be added to the menu?"

Max chuckled and a smile graced his face. He really was handsome in his own way. Yes, he had zero fashion sense, but his jaw was strong and angular and when he smiled, a tiny dimple appeared in his right cheek. It was barely visible under his two-day old stubble, but it was there, and his eyes were kind. She knew from high school that Max was fiercely loyal, and it radiated from every pore of his body but especially his eyes.

"I thought he was going to ground me for a week just for suggesting it." He laughed, and it was a deep, tingling laugh that sent a fluttering motion through her body. "I'm glad he didn't though or I would have had to sneak out to rescue you."

Layla's brow furrowed. "Rescue me? From what?"

Max's laugh quieted, and the light mood turned serious. "You don't remember?"

Layla thought back through high school memories. Many were a blur - she had tried to put them behind her - but suddenly one surfaced in her mind and she gasped. "Was that the same night as prom?"

Max nodded. "I wanted to ask you. I wish I had, but I don't think you really saw me in high school."

He was right about that. She hadn't really seen him. Of course, she'd known who he was. It was a small town and his father owned the only restaurant, but she didn't really know him. She'd been the newer girl in high school, having arrived late in her eighth-grade year - a hot commodity - and she had attracted the attention of several other boys, including Bruce Bollinger, the one who'd invited her to prom and then left her for a girl from a neighboring town. Was that why she felt so comfortable with Max? Because he'd swooped in and saved her asking nothing in return? And then his words connected in her mind. "You wanted to ask me to prom?"

Shock registered on his face as if he hadn't meant for that to slip out. His mouth opened and closed then opened again before he spoke. "Well, yeah, just to save you from that guy. I knew he was a jerk. I just didn't know he was *that* much of a jerk."

He was playing it off, but Layla could tell from his reaction that his explanation wasn't the whole truth. Had he liked her in high school then? How had she not seen what an amazing man he was? Amazing? Oh no, she could not be thinking like this. She had been engaged to marry someone else just a few weeks ago. She had sworn off men. She could not be falling for Max, could she?

No, she needed to change the subject now before she said something she might regret. "So, how about those menu ideas?"

She saw the look of disappointment flash across his face momentarily, but she couldn't help it. Falling for Max was just not something she should do right now. Not until she knew what she really wanted.

5

MAX

"Earth to Max. Are you going to put my order in?"

Max blinked, surprised to see Paula's hand waving in front of his face. He'd been thinking about the time with Layla last night. He couldn't believe he'd told her about his crush on her in high school. Even more, he couldn't believe she hadn't gone running. In fact, she had stayed until after ten. They'd reminisced about high school and laughed - she had the most angelic laugh like bells at Christmas. It was a laugh he could get used to hearing every day.

"Max! My order."

"Right." He cleared the thoughts from his mind. No use wandering down that road yet. He still had to get up the nerve to tell her how he felt. The moment had almost been there last night when he'd mentioned the dance. Her face had shifted just for a moment as if realizing his feelings. Before he could say anything though, she had switched the topic back to the menu, and the moment had been lost.

"Did something happen between you and Layla?" Paula asked in a teasing lilt. "You seem a little more preoccupied than normal."

Ned popped up from one of the booths. "Did you say something happened with Layla? Did you tell her how you feel?"

Max rolled his eyes and shook his head. "Nothing happened." He would have to be more careful at work or rumors would spread that they were on their way to marriage. Not that he'd mind marrying her, but that wasn't the way he wanted her to find out. He pushed open the kitchen door, grumbling about small town gossip under his breath.

"You say something, boss?" Carlos asked as he took the earbud out of his ear.

"Nothing important," Max said with a sigh. He handed over Paula's order and then his gaze landed on his notepad. He'd made a few more suggestions to the menu after Layla left. Perhaps now would be the perfect time to show her. "Actually, can you watch the diner for an hour or so?" It was their slow time with the breakfast rush over and the lunch rush a few hours off. Carlos should be fine to handle both the kitchen and the front for a bit.

"Sure thing, boss." Carlos removed his earbuds and deposited them in his pockets. Max appreciated how easygoing Carlos was. He could not have asked for a better employee. Perhaps he should see if Carlos had any family members who could help Layla out. He realized he didn't know much about his family but that could wait.

"Did you put my order in?" Paula asked as Max exited the kitchen.

"Yes. Carlos has it all under control. I'll be back in a bit."

"On your way to see Layla?" She sang the words more than said them, and he shook his head again, refusing to answer her.

The walk to the bed and breakfast was short. Most of the businesses in Star Lake were placed around downtown and on the main street in order to take advantage of the few travelers they did see. The bed and breakfast was on the opposite side of town from his diner but still within a ten-minute walk.

He didn't bother knocking. Layla's door was always open and she had told him more than once to come right in. Her voice carried through the small entryway as he stepped inside. Her words were muffled, but he could hear the strain in her voice.

"Randall, I don't know what to tell you. I don't have that book."

Max hung back a little. He didn't want to interrupt a

couple's spat, even if they weren't a couple any longer, but when he didn't hear Randall respond, he realized Layla was on the phone and Randall wasn't in the other room.

He stepped around the corner and Layla held up her hand as soon as she saw him. "Randall, I've got to go. I've got a customer. Look around your house. I'm sure you'll find it there." She placed the phone down and sighed. "Thank you. Your timing could not have been better."

"Everything okay?" Max asked.

"Fine," she said with a sigh. "Just Randall asking for some book he thinks he loaned me. It must have been his other fiancée though because I barely had time to read the wedding invitations much less a book."

Max looked down at the papers clutched in his hands. "I can come back if this is a bad time."

"No, it's fine. Let me just get Emma in here to watch the counter." She disappeared into the kitchen area and returned a moment later with a young blond girl. "You mind if we go out back? I could use a breath of fresh air."

Max followed her out the back door. The back of the bed and breakfast was surrounded by trees, making it feel even more isolated and quiet. A large wooden porch complete with chairs and a few tables in case patrons wanted to eat their meals outside filled the space, but Layla bypassed the chairs and leaned against the railing instead.

"I never thought breaking up would be so hard. Maybe it would have been better just to marry him."

Max placed his paper down and put a rock on top of it to keep it from blowing away. Then he placed his hands on her arms. "Don't say that. It's hard now, but you didn't love Randall. You deserve to be married to someone you love. Someone who loves you back. Someone who would do anything for you."

"I know, but where am I going to find someone like that?"

The world around them stopped. Not that it had been noisy before, but as their gazes locked, it was like all the birds and other things in nature had grown silent. He knew he shouldn't. She wasn't ready yet, but he couldn't stop his face from lowering to hers. As his lips touched hers, he knew that she was the only woman he wanted to kiss for the rest of his life. She was comfort, excitement, and love all rolled into one, and he knew no one else would ever come close.

For a moment, her body was stiff, but then she leaned into the kiss. Her hands grabbed the back of his neck, and her body pressed so close to his that he was no longer sure if the heartbeat he was feeling was his or hers. As suddenly as the kiss started though, it ended.

She pulled back and stared at him with wide eyes. "I have to go," she said in a soft voice before fleeing back into the safety of the bed and breakfast.

Great. Now what had he done?

❧ 6 ❧

LAYLA

Layla stared into the bottom of the ice cream container. Drat. She was out again, and she didn't want to venture out for fear of running into Max. It wasn't that she didn't want to see Max - no, that kiss had rocked her world - but she had no idea what to say to him. What did that kiss mean? She'd promised not to fall for any more men until she figured out what she wanted, but this was Max.

Yes, he was gruff on the outside and a little rough around the edges, but she knew there was a softer side inside. A sweet side. And that kiss had just proved it. But had he been kissing her because he cared or because he'd overheard her conversation with Randall and felt sorry for her?

Ugh, and then there was Randall. He'd called with the

book as an excuse, but the conversation had been laced with hurtful remarks about how she strung him along. Had she strung him along? She certainly hadn't meant to. Randall was a nice guy. A reliable guy. A boring guy. She groaned into her empty container. Maybe she had strung him along hoping he would open up and sweep her off her feet. The way the kiss with Max had.

A knock sounded at her door, and Layla stood, smoothing her shirt as she did. She didn't know why she bothered. The only person getting in that door was Kitty, and she didn't care how Layla looked. Kitty had been there when Layla canceled the wedding, she'd been there after prom when Bruce had left her for the other girl, and she would be here for her now. That's what friends were for, and Kitty was one of the best.

"Cat pajamas again?" Kitty asked when Layla opened the door.

Layla looked down at her pajama pants. Okay, maybe they were a little juvenile, but she couldn't help it. They were pink and purple and the cats were drinking coffee. She loved coffee. So much so that she was jonesing for her regular from Max's diner. She'd been avoiding it the last few days and making a pot at the bed and breakfast, but it was not the same. Not by a longshot.

She offered Kitty a shrug as she stepped back to let her in. "What can I say? I love cats and coffee. Please tell me you brought some coffee from Max's. This make-it-your-self stuff isn't cutting it."

Kitty held up her hands. In her left was a large dispos-able coffee cup and in her right was a bag from Max's. "Yes, I have your coffee and chocolate chip pancakes too. Max insisted. Are you going to tell me what happened between the two of you and why you're avoiding him and he looks like he hasn't slept in days?"

Layla sighed as she shut the door. "He kissed me. Or I kissed him. Or... I don't know who started it, but we kissed."

Kitty rolled her eyes. "Is that all? Why are you both acting like it's the end of the world?"

"Is that all? What do you mean is that all?" Layla took the coffee cup and tipped it back, enjoying the glorious flavors that exploded on her tongue. She continued to the kitchen, her stomach growling as the decadent scent of cinnamon and chocolate from the pancakes reached her nose. She was a decent cook, but nowhere near Max's level which was why she always snuck out and had breakfast at the diner instead of the bed and breakfast.

"I mean that he's had eyes for you since high school and you have a spot reserved in his diner. We've all been waiting for this to happen for years." She set the bag on the kitchen table and wandered to the fridge. Kitty was so comfortable in Layla's house that she never asked before raiding the fridge or the cupboards for food. "Good grief, Layla, what have you been eating?"

Layla blinked stupidly at her. Max had liked her in high school? Since high school? Was that why he had never married? Did she feel the same? It was true that she had staked out a table in his diner. She sat at it every morning and if ever someone was at the table, she would stare at them until they left. He'd tried to get her to sit at a different table, but she wanted none of it. That table allowed her to see him as he bustled behind the counter. It allowed her glimpses of him when he disappeared into the kitchen. Oh dear. She did like him too.

"Layla. Come in, Layla."

Layla shook her head at the sound of Kitty's fingers snapping. "What?"

"There you are. I asked what you've been eating. There is nothing in this fridge except a bottle of mustard." She held it up and wiggled it for effect.

What had she been eating? Ice cream, food from the bed and breakfast, she really had no idea. The images of food over the last few days were hazy at best.

"Are you okay?" Concern was etched in Kitty's wrinkled forehead and compassionate eyes.

"Yeah, I'm fine." Layla opened the bag and pulled out the container holding the pancakes. She flipped the lid open, her heart melting at the sight in front of her. Max had written "I'm sorry" on one of the pancakes and drawn a heart on the other along with a question mark. The corner of her lip pulled up as his quirky thoughtfulness swept over. Before she could stop herself, she blurted out, "I think I love him."

"Who?" Kitty asked. Layla had clearly shifted the conversation too quickly for her to catch up.

"Max."

Kitty rolled her eyes. "Of course you do. Glad you finally realize it, but why are you telling me? I'm not the one who needs to hear it."

"You're right." Layla glanced around for her keys, finally finding them under another empty tub of ice cream. "I have to tell him."

"You might want to change your pants first," Kitty said with a laugh as she pointed at Layla's bottom half.

Layla considered it for a moment, but what would be the point? If Max had liked her since high school, he'd already seen her highs and lows. Plus, if they did get together, he'd see her in these pants a lot. She might as well know now that he could handle it. No sense offering her heart to a man who would want her to change.

"You know what? I think I'm good." Kitty's laughter followed her out the door.

❧ 7 ❧

MAX

Max scowled as he scrubbed the counter. He shouldn't have kissed her. It was obviously too soon, but he'd been unable to stop it. However, now he wished he could turn back the hands of time and do it all over again. She hadn't been in the diner since the kiss, and he knew she was avoiding him. He'd rather have her as a friend than nothing at all.

His gaze wandered to the clock that sat above the door. He hated watches, especially while he was cooking, but knowing the time was a necessity. Especially on those days when Ned felt the desire to stick around and needle him with twenty questions. That man could get under his skin like no one else, but it was almost closing time and even Ned was gone for the day. He wondered though if Kitty had given Layla the food.

She'd only ordered coffee, but he knew from the order it was for Layla - no one else drank a coffee with two pumps of caramel and a squirt of hot fudge. He didn't even consider that coffee, but he'd wanted to do a little something to let her know he was thinking about her. Chocolate chip pancakes with an "I'm sorry" on one pancake in case she was mad and a heart and giant question mark on the other instead of the face had seemed to be the perfect way. Maybe she hadn't understood the question though. Maybe she was still trying to think of a way to let him down gently. She would definitely want to find the path of least conflict especially after the recent events with Randall.

The bell above the door jingled, bringing him out of his thoughts. It might be five minutes to closing time, but he was not making any more food tonight. "We're closed," he said, but when he lifted his eyes, the words died in his throat. Layla stood in his doorway.

"Should I leave then?" Her hand reached back for the door, but he could see the teasing glint in her eyes.

"Absolutely not, but I am going to lock it. It would be just my luck if Ned or Barnard showed up supposedly needing something after seeing you come in." Max hurried around the counter and locked the door, then pulled the blinds for good measure.

Then the awkward silence hit.

"I take it you got the pancakes." Why couldn't he say something more intelligent?

Nodding, she stepped toward him. "I did, and I wanted to say I'm sorry for running off and avoiding you the last few days."

He shook his head. "I'm the one who should apologize. You said you weren't ready for another relationship and then I just laid that kiss on you. I didn't mean to."

"Are you sorry you kissed me?"

She took another step closer, never averting her gaze. He loved her eyes, but he had no idea what to make of the way she was staring at him, like she was trying to see inside his soul. What should he say? If he told her the truth, would she run again? It didn't matter. He'd avoided the truth long enough, and he wasn't sure he could go back to pretending she didn't play a starring role in his thoughts all day long.

"No, I'm not sorry I kissed you. I've wanted to do that since prom night in high school."

Her eyes widened. "The night Bruce dumped me?"

"If not before." His voice sounded so strained in his ears; he was having trouble getting enough air to speak clearly.

"Why did you never tell me?" Her hand touched his arm, and heat licked all the way up to his shoulder.

"I didn't think you felt the same way, I thought it would ruin our friendship, you name it. Then, by the time I got up the nerve, you'd fallen in love with that other guy and moved away."

Her hand moved from his arm to his chest, and he swore his heart stopped beating for a moment. "I'm here now."

The way she said it sounded like an invitation. Then her face turned up, and he could see the desire in her eyes. It was more than he could take. "Yes, you are," he said, moments before his lips met hers again.

8

LAYLA

"Where are we going?" Layla asked as she watched the small town disappear out the passenger window of Max's truck. He'd asked her to accompany him to some unknown destination this afternoon, and as business was slow, she'd left her assistant in charge and agreed. Now, however, her curiosity was getting the best of her.

Max flashed her a crooked grin. "You'll see. You just need to be patient."

Patience was not one of her virtues, and she was pretty sure Max knew that. "You aren't really a serial killer, are you, taking me some place to hack me up?" She was kidding, simply trying to get a rise out of him, but he turned startled eyes on her.

"You have been watching too many horror flicks," he said before turning his attention back to the road ahead.

It was probably true. Layla was a huge movie buff, and generally watched something every night when she got off work. Her favorite movies were romantic comedies, but occasionally she shook it up with a western or a good horror flick.

"I'm just saying that Kitty knows I'm with you, and you know she'll send out a search party if I don't come back."

Max rolled his eyes and shook his head. "You'll be back in plenty of time tonight. Don't worry. In fact, if you keep annoying me, I might just turn the truck around now."

Layla smiled at the gruff tone that she knew was more bark than bite. He was simply teasing her back. Max almost never took an afternoon off, and he certainly wouldn't take her somewhere just to turn around and head back to Star Lake.

The truck slowed as Max turned down a wooded lane, and suddenly a cabin appeared.

"What is this?" Layla had no idea he had a cabin. The man almost never left the building he worked and lived in.

"This was my parent's cabin. When my dad left, he gave me the key." He parked the truck and turned off the engine.

"It's beautiful," Layla said, opening her door. Not only

was the cabin almost picturesque the way it was nestled into the trees, but the temperature outside was warm and balmy.

"I thought I could cook some dinner for you and teach you a little something."

"About cooking?" she asked.

"No, guitar." He lifted a black case from the back of the truck and headed toward the cabin door.

Layla blinked at him. "You play guitar?" She thought she'd known all there was to know about him, but he was full of surprises today.

"A little," he said with a soft smirk.

She followed him into the cabin, wondering if he knew of her secret love of guitarists. Some women fawned over men in uniform, but for her, a man with a guitar in his arms was one of the sexiest things she could think of. Add a cup of coffee and she'd probably be hooked for life.

The cabin was simple but nice. A large open area served as the living room with two couches, a table between them, and a fireplace across from them. Attached to it was a small kitchen and dining area, and upstairs was a single bedroom and bath.

"Are you hungry?" Max asked as he laid the guitar down on one of the couches. "I'm not sure I've stocked the place recently, but I'm sure there's some Mac n Cheese or canned food around.

Layla shook her head; she'd eaten before they left. "I

won't turn down a cup of coffee though if you have the fixings."

Max chuckled as he headed into the kitchen and began opening cupboard doors in search of coffee. "I almost brought some with me because I figured if you asked for anything, that would be it." He pulled out some grounds and an old pack of filters. "I don't have the crazy stuff you like though. It will have to be black with some sugar."

Ugh, she hadn't had regular black coffee in years. Even the few days she had avoided the diner, she'd doused her coffee with flavored creamer just to make it drinkable. Still, he was already making it, so she'd do her best to drink it. Perhaps if she poured in enough sugar it would mask the coffee taste.

"So, what made you want to come out here?" she asked as she took the cup he handed her.

He raised an eyebrow at her. "I love Star Lake, don't get me wrong, but people have a way of being in everyone's business there. I thought this way would be a little more relaxing."

Layla mashed her lips together to keep from laughing. It was a nice thought, but she would bet money that someone had seen them leave together and was already circulating a rumor. "They're good people, you know."

He nodded as he sipped on his coffee. She wanted to say more, something to get him to open up, but she wasn't sure what. He'd grown up there, and while she had spent most of her life there, he had certainly spent longer. Maybe the charm of a small town wore off with time, but she hoped not.

"So, when did you learn to play guitar and how did I not know about this?"

He set his cup down and opened the guitar case. "My dad played a little, and he tried to teach me in high school, but I didn't really want to learn. When you left and then he left," he shrugged as he pulled the instrument out, "I thought it might be time to learn."

"But who taught you?" Max hated technology. The man didn't even have a watch or carry a cell phone. She was fairly certain he didn't have a computer where he could pull up online tutorial videos.

His fingers strummed the strings. "Turns out I'm kind of a natural. I guess I remembered a few things my dad had taught me and then I sort of taught myself the rest."

She watched as the fingers of his left hand moved deftly across the struts as his right picked the strings. The sound that came out of the guitar was nothing like what she would have thought Max would play. Soft and gentle, it was almost a complete opposite of him.

"You want to learn?" He stopped suddenly, and she wondered if he had mistaken her staring for interest.

"No, I'm no good at any instrument. My mother tried to get me to take piano lessons when I was younger, but I refused to cut my nails and therefore was a terrible student. Don't get me started on the recorder incident."

Max chuckled and moved to sit next to her on the couch. "You might be surprised." He plucked the coffee from her hand and placed it on the table. Then he set the instrument in her hands.

The wood felt smooth and heavier than she'd expected. The strings were rough against her fingers. "How do you do this? I feel like the strings are going to cut the skin of my fingers."

"You build up to it," he said with a soft smile. "Calluses are a hazard of the job." He reached an arm behind her to help position her fingers correctly, and Layla breathed in his scent. She could care less about learning guitar, but if it brought him this close to her, she would fake her interest.

When her fingers were in place, she strummed with her right hand, producing a sound nowhere near as nice as the one he had. "Like this?" She turned to look up at him and realized his face was inches from hers. Close enough to kiss if either of them moved more than an inch.

His eyes closed and she shut hers preparing for the touch of his lips. And then her phone rang. Max pulled back and she opened her eyes, sighing as she extricated the phone from her pocket.

"Trouble?" Max asked as she viewed the display.

"Probably." She'd told Emma not to call her unless it

was an emergency. The girl better be serious. She tapped the button to answer the call.

"Layla? It's Emma. I'm soooo sorry to bother you, but I think the fridge just went out. The light inside is dark, and I'm afraid all of the food is going to spoil."

Layla sighed and shot Max an apologetic look. "Okay, Emma, thanks for calling. I'll be there in an hour."

"Guess that guitar lesson will have to wait." Max took the guitar as she hung up the phone.

"I'm sorry. Emma thinks our fridge went out. I'm hoping she's wrong, but I need to check and take care of the food before it spoils."

He placed the guitar back in the case and snapped it closed. "I have some extra room in the freezer at the diner if you need it."

Layla flashed him a thankful smile. "I may just take you up on that."

9

MAX

Max was saddened that his time with Layla had been cut short, but the bed and breakfast was her business. He couldn't fault her for wanting to take care of it; he would have done the same had it been the fridge in his diner. Still, he wondered when they might be able to steal a few moments away together again.

The festival was quickly approaching, and they still had planning to do which would throw them together, but he wanted time with her to just relax, to enjoy her company. He wanted the opportunity to show her they belonged together.

He turned the lock on the diner door and flipped the sign to closed. Perhaps he could make some time tomorrow to bring her an early lunch. Satisfied with that idea, he clicked the lights off and headed for the stairs to his apartment, but the ringing of the diner phone halted his progress.

Max abhorred cell phones and how tethered they made people, so he didn't own one. The diner had a landline as did his apartment, but almost no one called the diner's line. No one except his father. He thought about letting the call go to the old answering machine his father had installed, but what if his father was hurt? It seemed the man never called without a reason. With a sigh, Max picked up the phone. "Hello?"

"Max." Just the sound of his name from his father's lips brought back memories he didn't want to face - memories of his mother's death and the fights with his father afterwards - but he forced himself to be civil. He was older now, a grown man who no longer had to do what his father told him.

"What do you need, Dad?" Dad. The word felt forced and dirty in his mouth. His father hadn't been a dad in years, but somehow Max couldn't call him any other name. At one time, he and his father had been close, but after his mother had died … things had changed.

"I need your help. I broke my leg, and I need someone to help me out around the apartment for a few days until I can get on my feet again."

Max ran a hand across the back of his neck. He didn't need this. Not now. Yes, Carlos could probably handle the diner for a few days, but this thing with Layla had just started. Plus, there was the festival he needed to help plan, but this was his father. While they hadn't been close in the last few years, could he really tell his father no?

"Okay, Dad, let me pack a few things, and I'll head your way."

There was a pause long enough that Max wondered if the old man had hung up on him. Finally, his father's voice came over the line. "Thank you, son. I appreciate it."

Max grunted in acknowledgement and managed a gruff goodbye before hanging up the phone. His dad might appreciate it now, but after they spent the next few days at each other's throats, he doubted his father would feel the same way.

He dialed Carlos before heading upstairs to pack a small bag. Thankfully Carlos was one of those rare gems - he never seemed to mind pitching in where he could and he agreed to run the diner for the few days Max was gone. At least that was one thing off his mind.

With his bag packed and the diner taken care of, Max contemplated calling Layla. Even though it was late, he knew she would probably be awake, but what would he say? He hated that he was leaving her without much of an explanation, but he just didn't feel like getting into an emotional discussion about his dad right now. No, Carlos could fill her in tomorrow morning.

He was being cowardly and he knew it, but it didn't change his mind as he loaded up his old truck and pulled away from the diner. No doubt someone had seen him leave with his bag and would start the rumors flying, but that could wait for another day.

10

LAYLA

Layla couldn't fight the grin that tugged the corners of her mouth up as she made her way into Max's diner. She'd been disappointed she had to cut their time short yesterday, but thankfully, the fridge hadn't been broken; it had just come out of the outlet slightly. She had no idea how that had happened, but she would take the blessing. Visitors had been fewer this year, and she did not have the savings to replace major appliances. She just wished it hadn't taken her so long to figure it out. Had she realized the problem sooner, perhaps she could have still managed some time with Max last night.

She pulled open the door and glanced around for him, but he was nowhere in sight. Probably helping Carlos in the kitchen; he did that often when the breakfast rush hit, but when she saw Kitty waving her over as if flagging down a rescue chopper, her heart froze. Kitty was often dramatic and animated - it was one thing Layla loved about her - but she was a horrible poker player. Whatever she thought somehow displayed on her face, and right now Layla was reading that she had a big, awful secret. One that Layla would not enjoy.

"Did you hear Max left last night?" Kitty whispered when Layla slid into her seat.

"He did what?" She'd been prepared to hear that Barnard was raising taxes again or maybe that Ned was picketing to have a chicken crosswalk - anything that might cost her more money - but she had not been expecting those words.

Kitty's blue eyes were wide as she nodded so vigorously that her ringlet curls bounced on either side of her head. "Yep. Paula said she saw him leave the diner with a suitcase last night, load up his truck, and take off." She lowered her voice and glanced around as if the next part was too juicy to be said aloud. "No one has seen him this morning."

Max couldn't have left. He wouldn't have left without telling her, would he? They'd had such a nice time yesterday, and she'd thought they were connecting. Had he been angry she'd had to cut their time short? No, that wasn't Max. He was grumpy and maybe a little snarky sometimes, but she'd never seen him really angry over anything. Not since she'd known him.

"He wouldn't have just left the diner." Layla wasn't sure if she was trying to convince Kitty or herself. "Has anyone asked Carlos?"

Kitty shook her head. "I don't know. I only got here a moment ago. Just long enough to hear the scuttlebutt from Paula."

"Well, I'm going to find out." Layla stood and made her way toward the kitchen. She could feel every eye in the place on her, but she wasn't going to let that stop her. Max never let anyone in the kitchen, and she wasn't even sure he would have let her in had he been here, but he wasn't here and she needed answers.

Taking a deep breath, she pushed open the swinging door. Carlos looked up at her with wide eyes. "What are you doing in the kitchen?" he asked as he made his way toward her, shaking his head with every step. "Mr. Max says no one is allowed in the kitchen. Not even you."

His words stung but not as much as the fact that Max had left without telling her. "Where did he go, Carlos?"

"He said he had some business with his dad. Asked me to run the diner for a few days. That's all I know." He shooed her with his hands. "Now you have to get out of the kitchen."

Layla nodded and walked back to the table where Kitty sat, waiting to hear what she'd learned. His father. She knew they'd had a rocky relationship since his mother died, and she could only imagine it had to have been something big if Max would leave the diner.

"Well?" Patience was not Kitty's virtue either.

"He went to see his dad."

"Oh." All of the excitement had left Kitty's voice. "That's not very exciting."

No, it wasn't exciting, but it was troubling. Why wouldn't he have told her? But then she realized what she'd never taken the time to consider before. She hadn't been here for Max when he'd had other huge life changes. She hadn't been there for him when his mother died or when he and his father had fought over the diner. Nor had she been there when his father left town. It was no wonder he hadn't clued her in now. She had missed so much of his life with the years she had been away from Star Lake, and he'd probably had no one to confide in.

Her mind wandered back to Jed, the man she had followed out of Star Lake after high school. She'd thought he loved her, but after uprooting her life for him, he'd withdrawn and stopped talking with her. Their marriage had quickly staled as if they were mere roommates and not a couple. She had tried everything to make it work, but after a few years, she had accepted defeat and signed the dotted line before returning to Star Lake. Was this her Karma? Had Max realized she couldn't live up to the image he had created in high school?

Suddenly, her cell phone began ringing. She quickly pulled it out of her pocket to silence the annoying ring tone. She'd had no plans to answer it, but when she saw the name on the caller ID, she punched the answer button and headed for the door.

"Hello?"

"Layla Montgomery? This is Ellie Winston with Homestead Hotels."

Ellie Winston. Layla hadn't thought she would ever hear that name again. She had applied for a general manager position months ago when she'd thought she'd be marrying Randall and moving to the city, but she hadn't expected to hear back from the woman. And she'd certainly forgotten all about the application. Until now.

"Hello, Ms. Winston, what can I do for you?"

"Actually, it's what I can do for you."

11

MAX

"Dad, seriously, sit down. I'll get it." Max wasn't sure why his father asked him to come if he was just going to try and do everything himself. "You're supposed to be taking it easy."

"I'm sorry," his father grumbled as he plopped back down in the kitchen chair. "I've been on my own for so many years now that I'm not used to having to be still."

Max knew the words weren't meant as a dig, but they felt that way all the same. He knew his father had been on his own for the last several years after the death of Max's mother. Perhaps he should have tried harder to swallow his pride and visit his father more often.

"Who's watching the diner?" his father asked as Max set down a plate of scrambled eggs and bacon in front of him.

"My cook, Carlos. He's good, but I'll check in on him in a minute. The breakfast rush usually lasts until eleven, so he'll be pretty busy until then." Max set his own plate down and took the chair across from his father.

His father took a bite of the eggs, but Max could tell from his thoughtful expression that he had more questions. "Is it just the two of you then?"

"It's a small town, Dad. Two of us can handle the diner efficiently." He took a sip from his coffee wondering just where his father was going with this.

There was a slight pause as his father pushed the eggs around on his plate. "But that makes it hard for you to take time off, doesn't it?"

Max chuffed and shook his head. "I don't need to take time off. What would I do?"

"I don't know. Maybe date." Concern brimmed in his father's eyes as he held Max's gaze.

Ah, so that's what this was about. His father was concerned he would end up alone, maybe die before having children to leave the diner to. "For your information, I had a date yesterday."

"That's good. How did it go?" Though the question was nonchalant, Max could tell his father was more than just curious.

"It went well until she had to cut the day short to deal with a problem at her job." Max wondered if Layla had been forced to purchase a new fridge. He probably should have called her before leaving town.

"And are you planning to see her again?"

Max sighed and set his fork down, piercing his father with a penetrating gaze. "What's with the third degree, Dad?"

"I just want you to be happy. Your mom and I had a long happy life together before she passed. My wish is the same for you."

"I'm working on it, Dad, but it does take two. I'm trying to give her enough space to be sure this is what she wants."

His father's brow arched. "Space or distance?"

Max finished his eggs and pushed back from the table. "I need to check on Carlos."

It was the few moments like these that Max wished he had a cell phone. Without one, he was at the mercy of his father's landline which also happened to be located in the kitchen where his father still sat.

He dialed the number he knew by heart and turned his back to his father. The phone rang four times before a breathless Carlos answered. "Hello? Max's Diner."

"Carlos, It's Max. How is everything going?"

"Business is okay, boss, but your leaving sure raised a lot of questions. There's a rumor floating around that you left. You are coming back, right?"

It was the first time he had ever heard worry in

Carlos's voice, and he hurried to assure him. "Yes, Carlos. I am coming back as soon as I know my dad can take care of himself." He paused unsure if he should ask the question burning in his mind. "Did Layla come in this morning?"

A long pause stretched out before Carlos answered. "She did, and she didn't seem happy, boss. I told her where you were; I hope that's okay. You didn't say I couldn't, and she's kind of intense sometimes."

Max chuckled at the tremor of fear in Carlos's voice. He'd seen the intensity Carlos spoke of and could understand the man's hesitation. "Yeah, it's fine you told her. Was she mad?"

"She certainly wasn't happy, but I don't know how mad she was because she left without ordering."

That wasn't like Layla at all. "She left?"

"Yeah, she took a phone call outside and never came back in."

Okay, that was worrisome. Had the incident with her fridge been worse than he'd thought? Had Randall reappeared in her life? "Okay, thanks, Carlos. I'll see you soon." Max hung up the phone and pondered what he should do.

"Trouble?" his father asked from the table.

Max turned to face his father. "Maybe." He paused and studied his father. He couldn't believe the offer he was about to propose, but what other choice did he have? If he stayed here, he might lose Layla and that wasn't an option. "What would you say if I asked you to come and stay with me until you're back on your feet?"

His father ran a hand along his chin as he regarded Max. "You'd let me stay with you?"

"Yes." Max took a deep breath hoping he wouldn't regret his words. "But only IF you promise not to badger me about the diner. It's fine the way it is, and I don't want to fight with you about it."

The two men traded stares as his father thought about the offer. Finally, he nodded. "Deal."

12

LAYLA

Layla stared at the offer Ellie Winston had sent over. It wasn't the general manager position she had originally applied for, but it paid substantially more than she made running the inn here and it held the opportunity to climb the ranks and achieve even more. Of course, it was still dependent on an interview, but Ellie had assured her that was more formality than anything.

Could she really leave Star Lake again though? She'd left once - for Jed - and it hadn't turned out well, but this time she would be leaving for herself. But did she want to? Yes, she was frustrated Max had left without telling her, but she also understood why he had. Plus, she felt that whatever was blossoming between them was real. Could she leave knowing Max would never leave Star Lake?

On the other hand, could she afford not to? Bookings at

the inn had been lower this year for whatever reason, and money was getting tight. Taking this job would allow her to earn some and squirrel it away for when she returned.

Before she could focus more on it, the door to the inn opened and Max strode in.

"Are you okay?" Layla asked as she came around the desk and approached him. She wanted to throw her arms around him, but she was still a little hurt that he'd left without telling her.

He had the decency to look sheepish as he nodded. "I am. My father broke his leg and needed some help. I'm sorry I didn't call you before I left; I should have."

"Yes, you should have," Layla said with a smile, "but I think I know why you didn't." She was about to continue when her cell phone rang. She pulled it out and sighed when she saw her sister's name. "Hold that thought," she said to Max as she answered the call, turning slightly to give herself a modicum of privacy.

"Bella? What's wrong?" Bella was her younger sister, and while Layla didn't always have her life figured out, Bella rarely seemed to. The girl had been flighty all her life, but when she'd graduated high school, it had gotten even worse. Always a dreamer, Bella jumped from one idea to the next before the first one truly had time to blossom, and her track record with men was almost as bad.

When Bella had married Mark a year ago, Layla had hoped that he might be able to ground her. Mark was solid, stable, an investment banker in a large firm. The Yin to Bella's Yang. They were about as opposite as a couple could be, but somehow it worked for them.

Bella's voice was high-pitched and frenzied as she answered. "It's the baby, Layla. I think something's wrong. Mark is on a business trip, so I can't call him, but something is not right. Can you come?"

Bella was also eight months pregnant - an excuse she had used to avoid attending Layla's almost wedding a few weeks ago. In reality, it was probably a mixture of the fact that Bella had been at her first wedding and was often forgetful of things that didn't directly involve her. While Layla could not wait to see her niece, there was a part of her that truly hoped the kid took more after her father than her mother.

"Bella, it's okay. What's wrong?" Layla had never been pregnant, and she probably would have no idea how to help Bella anyway, but she could be a voice of reason for her sister if nothing else. Sometimes, a level head was all Bella needed.

"I don't know. I'm having really sharp pains, and I haven't felt her kick all day."

Layla took a deep breath. Bella only lived a few hours away, but she wasn't sure a road trip was really necessary. "Bella, can you get to your doctor or the hospital? Can you drive?"

"I think so. Why?"

Layla glanced back to Max to apologize that this was taking longer than she expected, but he was gone. She fought back a sigh. She'd find him as soon as she finished here and apologize. "I want you to get to the doctor or the hospital and have them check you. My gut is that you are having Braxton Hicks contractions-"

"What are those?" Bella asked, interrupting Layla.

"False labor pains, but the doctors know for sure. If it's something serious, call me back, and I promise I'll head your way. Okay?"

"Okay." The one word was more of a tremulous sigh than a confident assurance, but Layla knew she could do it.

After issuing her goodbye and final words of assurance to her sister, Layla ended the call, informed Emma she would be back momentarily, and went in search of Max.

M ax looked up as the branches of the willow tree parted. Layla had found him as he figured she would.

"Sorry about that. It was Bella. You know how she gets sometimes." She sat beside him and pulled her knees to her chest.

"Is she okay?" Max hadn't known Bella as well as Layla, but he was aware of her dramatic personality.

"I think so. She's pregnant - I don't know if I told you that - and freaking out because she's having pains and hasn't felt the baby move. Mark is out of town, and she wants me to come, but I told her it was probably Braxton Hicks. I told her to get checked out by a doctor and call me if it was something serious."

Max nodded and a silence fell between them. "I brought my father back with me."

Layla turned to look at him. "You did? How's that going to go?"

"I don't know, but I couldn't leave him there alone and I knew I had to get back. For the diner." He plucked at a blade of grass before meeting her eyes. "And for you."

"Max-"

He held up his hand to cut her off. "Let me finish before I lose the courage to tell you this. Layla, I've loved you since high school. There has never been another woman for me. I know I'm stubborn and opinionated and probably hard to live with, but I also know that my life isn't complete without you in it. That kiss we shared rocked my world, and I can't go back to just being friends. Maybe I messed it up by leaving without telling you, but I didn't want to drag you into issues with my father. However, I know that was wrong, and the only way for us to make this work is to share everything. You said you were swearing off men, and I wanted to give you time, but I can't let another day go by without telling you that I love you."

He closed his mouth to keep any more rambling words from spilling out. Though it was hard, he would wait for Layla's response. If she no longer wanted to see him, it might kill him, but at least he would know for sure.

Layla pursed her lips for a moment and then shook her

head. "Max, I had no idea that you felt that way about me all these years. I've been stupid and blind, but I love you too. It was obvious from the moment we kissed. Yes, I wish you would have told me where you were going, but only because I wanted to be there for you." She laid a hand on his arm. "Being in a relationship means sharing everything together. The good and the bad."

"You're right. I'm not very good at this relationship thing, but I'd like to learn."

"We can learn together." Layla pulled her knees underneath her and leaned over until her face was inches from his. Their gazes locked, emotion flowing between them like an invisible current before she closed her eyes and placed her mouth on his.

All of his fears and frustrations fizzled with the heat that burned between them, and he forced himself to pull back before he lost all control.

"I will never get tired of kissing you," he said, running a thumb across her lips. He expected a smile, and concern flooded him when her eyes shifted to the side. "What is it?"

Sighing, Layla sat back. "I got a call from a lady yesterday. She wants me to interview for a management job."

Max's brow furrowed in confusion. "I don't understand. You have a job. Here."

Layla's lips folded in and mashed together. "I do, but

the inn isn't bringing in money like I thought it would. Maybe if I take this job, I can earn enough to put some away. That way when I return, I'll have some money to cover even when times are tough."

He didn't want her to go. In fact, he wanted to scream at her to stay. They were just getting started. They had just admitted their love for each other. Why would she want to go now? But he knew why. Being able to take care of herself was her "thing." His "thing" was running the diner. Always had been. It was why he stayed in Star Lake. It was why a wedge had been driven between him and his father over the running of it, but Layla needed more. She needed to prove that she could take care of herself even though he could take care of them both.

"You know if you need money…" He didn't get to finish the statement before her finger was on his lips and her head was shaking back and forth.

"No, Max. I could never take your money. I know this is awful timing, but I have to do this. I have to be able to make it on my own. I married Jed because I was scared to stay here alone. I almost married Randall for the same reason. If I really want this to work between us, and I do, then I need to be sure I can stand by myself first."

He nodded though inside his heart was breaking. Had he just bared his heart only to get it trampled again?

14

LAYLA

Layla stepped out of the cab and stared up at the impressive building. It was larger than anything in Star Lake, stretching up nearly to the clouds, but it also had none of the charm of the smaller buildings in Star Lake. She swallowed a sigh and smoothed her skirt.

Skirts were rarely in her wardrobe rotation in Star Lake; nobody there cared if she wore jeans and flowered shirts to work every day. She'd had to scavenge her closet for this one, and the fit was snugger than she would have liked. Probably all those chocolate chip pancakes. Add that to the heels she never wore, and her walk up to the front door was stiff at best, comical more than likely.

Squaring her shoulders to try and summon courage, she pulled open the glass doors. The inside of the building was simple, elegant, classy. And boring. There were no odd pieces of art decor like Paula had hanging in her ballet studio. There were no old-time posters like Max had adorning the walls of the diner. There weren't even kitschy paintings like the ones in the bed and breakfast. No, here the walls were a smooth sand color just slightly darker than the floor, and the only pops of color were the few abstract art paintings spaced evenly apart and sparsely around the room. It was completely devoid of personality.

Could she actually come work here every day? She, the woman people said, had a personality larger than life? Suddenly, she wasn't sure.

"Can I help you?" The woman behind the desk not only had a nasally voice that barely disguised her annoyance, but she couldn't even be bothered to stop tapping away on her computer screen and look Layla in the eye.

"Yes, I'm Layla Montgomery, and I'm here for an interview with Ellie Winston." Her own voice sounded timid to her ears, and Layla forced a smile to her face in an effort to portray more confidence than she felt.

The woman spared her only a passing glance before tapping the headset on the side of her head and punching a button on the phone. "Mrs. Winston, your appointment is here." There was a pause and then she tapped the headpiece once more. "Have a seat. She'll be right out."

Layla nodded and took a seat in one of the chairs. The chair looked beautiful with its cream-colored upholstery, but it was the least comfortable chair she had ever sat in. Did no one try these out before ordering them? Every piece of furniture in the bed and breakfast had been sat upon multiple times by both herself and Kitty before it had been purchased. Layla wanted to be sure her guests were comfortable no matter where they chose to sit.

"Layla, so glad you could make it." Ellie Winston was a petite woman with a perfect figure and a pointy chin. Her blond hair was pulled back so tightly on her head that Layla was pretty sure she was giving herself a facelift and a headache at the same time.

"Thanks for inviting me." Layla held out her hand to shake, but Ellie simply lifted an eyebrow and blinked at her. Embarrassed, Layla dropped her hand and decided to let Ellie give the cues. Evidently interactions here were very different than in Star Lake too.

"If you'll follow me, we'll get the interview started." Ellie whirled in a single motion and led the way down another bland hallway to an equally boring door. She pushed it open, and Layla felt as if someone had punched her in the gut.

She'd thought she would just be having an interview with Ellie, but there were nine other perfect faces staring expectantly at her.

"You may sit here." Ellie pointed to the chair at the head of the table. A bottle of water and a sheet of paper sat on the table. "The water is for you, of course. The paper is a list of our questions. We'll give you a moment to go over them, and then we'll take turns asking the questions."

Layla nodded, but her throat constricted as she realized each person around the table had their own set of questions and a pen. None of them looked friendly. Not a smile could be found on any face.

She pulled out the chair and scanned the questions. What management experience did she have? Why did she want to work for Homestead Hotels? What would she do if she had an unruly customer? How would she handle noise complaints from other occupants? Most of the questions seemed straightforward. Not that she had many of these issues in her bed and breakfast, but they did crop up occasionally. However, it was the last question that gave her pause. Where did she see herself in five years? She knew the answer they wanted to hear - something about climbing the ladder or owning a hotel - but that wasn't her answer. Married to Max was where she saw herself in five years. Maybe with a kid on the way.

"I'm sorry, I think I've made a mistake." Layla set the paper down and pushed back her chair. "I'm sure this is a wonderful opportunity, but I like my small town. I like being able to wear jeans to work if I want, and I love the quirky people I get to deal with on a daily basis. As wonderful as this sounds, I don't think I'd be happy here, and I don't want to waste our time any further."

Before any of the stiff people in the room could utter a

response, Layla strode out the door, down the hallway, and past the nasally receptionist. A sense of uplifting freedom hit her when she exited the stuffy building, and she knew that as hard as it might be financially, she had made the right decision.

She called the taxi company she had used to arrive and placed an order for a return to the airport. As soon as she ended that call, her phone rang again. Her heart leapt with the hope it might be Max, but it was her sister's voice that came through the device.

"Layla? Can you talk?"

Layla was relieved to hear her sister's voice no longer held the frantic edge it had the day before, but she could not help the disappointment that flowed through her that she wasn't Max. "Yes, I'm free. Is everything okay? Did you go to the doctor's?"

"I did, and you were right. It was just Braxton Hicks. I wanted to tell you thank you and sorry that I worried you."

"That's what sisters are for, Bella. Now, you better call me when it's really time. I want to be there for the birth of my niece."

"I will."

15

MAX

M ax was just closing up when the front door flew open and Layla burst in.

"What are you doing here? I thought you had an interview at Homestead Hotels?"

Her lips broke into a wide smile. "I did, but when I got there, I realized I couldn't work there."

"Oh yeah? Why's that?" He set down the rag he had been cleaning the counters with and took a step toward her.

"It was boring for one." She took a step closer.

He tilted his head. "Boring? The job?" He edged forward a bit more

"No, the building although probably the job would have been as well. There was no personality on the walls or in the people who worked there." Another step closed the distance, and she stood before him. "But that wasn't the biggest reason."

"No?" His heart pounded in his chest as he scanned her face.

She shook her head, her soft hair bouncing against her shoulders. "No. The real reason I couldn't work there is because you weren't there." She placed a hand on his chest and heat flared beneath it. "I realized all the money in the world didn't matter if I didn't have you there with me."

"I would have sold the diner to be with you." Though they were true, hearing himself say the words out loud surprised him.

Layla smiled and moved her hands to behind his neck. "Yeah, but then how would I get my coffee and chocolate chip pancakes every morning?"

He would cook for her wherever, but he could tell from the look in her eyes that she'd been teasing. It was her way of deflecting his serious words. "That is true. How on earth would I make your favorites without this diner?"

"Speaking of which, I'm starving. Do you think I could get some pancakes?"

Max chuckled, but there was no way he was letting go of her until he got a kiss. "I'll make you pancakes as soon as you pay for them. Your tab is getting a little out of control."

"Then I guess I better do something about that." She lifted the final few inches separating their faces and their lips met. Max had thought the other kisses were the best in his life, but they held no candle to this one. Fire and passion brimmed beneath the surface, and every fear and longing the two of them had been trying to stuff down erupted between them. Max knew he would never tire of kissing her. Not even if he did it every day for the rest of his life which was his plan.

When the kiss ended, he fired up the grill and began mixing the ingredients for Layla's pancakes. "You know, we're going to have to spend a lot of time together over the next few weeks to be ready for the festival." He glanced at her out of the corner of his eye as he mixed the ingredients together.

"That we will," she said before grabbing a chocolate chip and popping it in her mouth. "It's a good thing Emma is competent enough to handle the bed and breakfast for a few hours."

"Carlos as well," Max said with a smile.

Suddenly there was a thumping sound on the stairs. Layla looked at him with wide eyes, but Max merely shook his head. "Here, watch the pancakes for a second." He handed her the spatula before exiting the kitchen.

He met his father halfway on the staircase. The man was clutching the railing and breathing heavily. "Dad? What are you doing? You're supposed to be taking it easy."

"I was, but then I got hungry. You have no food in that

fridge upstairs, so I thought I'd come down and whip something up." He paused and sniffed the air. "From the smell of it, you've already started."

"Layla is here, and I'm making her pancakes." He wrapped an arm around his father and helped him down the last few steps.

"For dinner?" Max's father had never been a fan of breakfast for dinner.

Max chuckled. "For every meal she can." They reached the level floor, and after making sure his father was situated, Max headed back to the kitchen. "I better check on her before she burns the place down."

"I heard that," came her voice from the kitchen.

Smiling, he pushed open the door to see her wielding the spatula and flipping the pancakes with ease. "I thought you said you didn't cook." She'd always told him that Emma did most of the cooking at the bed and breakfast.

Chagrin covered her face, and she offered a small shrug. "So I cook. A little. But you do it so much better."

"You better be glad I don't mind cooking for you," he said with a smile as she placed the pancakes on a plate.

"Think an old man could get some of those too?" his father asked as he hobbled into the kitchen.

"Dad, you hate breakfast for dinner," Max said.

His father nodded. "I do, but I don't mind pancakes for a late-night snack."

Layla laughed and handed the plate to him. "Here you

go, Mr. Gibson. I'm sure there's enough batter left to make a few more."

"First off, call me Leo. Secondly, don't you two have some planning to do? You take those pancakes and eat. I'm capable of whipping up a few more for myself."

Layla glanced to Max, giving him the final say. He looked back at his father. Walking around on his leg wasn't good for him, but pancakes didn't require standing for long. "Okay, Dad, but only if you promise to sit down afterwards and rest your leg."

"I promise. Now you too get out there and do what you need to do." He took the spatula from Layla and proceeded to shoo them out of the kitchen with it.

"You know, you might not get your kitchen back," Layla whispered as they headed for a table.

Max looked back at the swinging doors. He'd thought he would hate having his father here, but so far, it hadn't been that bad. He hadn't realized how much time had passed between them or how much he had missed having family around, but he also knew his father wouldn't stay. As much as he might talk about his time running the diner, Max knew he was enjoying retirement, and now that the two had made a promise to keep in touch more often, he would enjoy it even more. "I don't think that will be an issue."

Layla tilted her head and fixed him with a questioning gaze.

Max chuckled. "Let's just say we talked a lot on the drive down here."

"I'm glad." She took a bite of her pancake and swallowed. "And I'm sorry. That I wasn't here when your mother died or your father left the first time. I promise that I'll be here for any other big events in your life."

He placed his hand over her free one and smiled. "We'll both be here. Together."

EPILOGUE

LAYLA

The day of their turn to host the festival dawned warm and bright as had every day that week. It was like God was smiling down on their little town and blessing them with warmth and sunlight. And a lot of tourists. Somehow, Barnard had managed to get the festival advertised in surrounding towns, and tourists had filled the town every day for the last week. Today was no exception.

Layla couldn't believe how perfect it was turning out. Though she usually found Barnard's ideas frustrating and time consuming, she had to admit this one had been a success. Barnard's ice cream shop had been overflowing yesterday, and Kitty had worked non-stop cutting hair and making new clients. And now, her bed and breakfast was filled with new faces.

People wandered through the bed and breakfast, oohing and aahing over the rooms, the food, and the ambiance. Even Bella and Mark had made the drive out with Baby Nicole, who was probably the most beautiful baby that Layla had ever seen. Currently Bella sat in one of the recliners, rocking the sleeping angel and smiling at everyone who stopped to admire the baby.

"I can't believe one of his ideas actually worked out," Max said as he plated up another round of burgers for the dining room.

"Yeah, business has definitely picked up this week, and I've already received bookings through Christmas and into next year. I'm so glad I didn't sell the bed and breakfast."

"Me too." Max leaned in to place a kiss on her lips before heading out of the kitchen to deliver the food. He had been working so hard, first making breakfasts for everyone and now lunch. She knew he had some pasta creation planned for dinner. Though he wasn't getting paid much for today, she had no doubt his business would pick up as well after today. Thankfully, his father had come back into town to help for the day, and the two were taking turns at the stove.

"Excuse me, can you tell me where I can find Layla?"

Layla looked up to see a vaguely familiar young woman with mostly blond hair except for one solitary streak of purple staring at her. Though not everyone could pull the look off, it worked on this girl. "I'm Layla. What can I do for you?"

She held up a basket overflowing with pastries. "I'm Presley Hays. I don't know if you remember me, but I used to live here before taking a job in Paris. Anyway, I just bought the old laundromat and am converting it into a bakery. I was hoping to have it done in time to participate in this event, but I'm a little behind." She bit her lip. "Still, I was hoping maybe I could put out some of my pastries and some cards in case people wanted to come back later?"

It wasn't really a question, but the girl's voice rose at the end as if unsure of Layla's answer or if she should even be posing the question. Never one to turn down a sweet, Layla studied the contents of the basket. It was over-flowing with muffins, croissants, and other baked goods. Her eyes lit up when she spied what looked like an apple cinnamon muffin. Next to chocolate chip pancakes, they were her favorite food. "I'll tell you what, if I can taste that apple cinnamon thing there first, then I'll be happy to let you put the treats out wherever you'd like."

Presley's eyes lit up. "Really? Yes, of course, here you go." She scooped the apple cinnamon muffin up and held it out to Layla.

The tantalizing aroma hit Layla as soon as she opened the Saran wrapping. Smiling, she held the pastry below her nose and sniffed before taking a bite. She loved the smell of cinnamon and apples together.

Peeling back the wrapping carefully, she took a tentative bite. Flavors exploded in her mouth, and she nodded at Presley, forcing herself not to devour the rest of the muffin in two bites. "This is delicious, Presley. I don't think you'll have any issues selling these."

The woman's face lit up. "Really? Thank you so much." With that, the younger woman spun on her heel and headed toward the dining area.

A moment later, Max returned, a furrowed expression on his brow. "Did you tell some girl she could put out muffins?"

Layla chuckled and took his hand. "I did. Her name is Presley Hays. Evidently, she used to live in Star Lake, and now she's back. She bought the old laundromat and is opening up a bakery."

"She better not sell sandwiches that would steal my customers," Max grumbled as he glanced toward the dining room.

Layla placed her hand on his cheek. "Don't worry. Your burgers are what people come in for anyway, and no one will ever compete with you on those."

His arms encircled her waist. "Those and my chocolate chip pancakes, right?" A tiny dimple popped in his cheek as his lips pulled into a smile.

Layla wrapped her other hand behind his neck and returned his grin. "Of course. I'll be needing those every day for the rest of my life."

"I think we can make that happen."

Max's eyes closed, and moments later his lips were on hers. Heat flooded her body, and she knew that he was the man she wanted to kiss for the rest of her life.

"Layla, have you tasted these?" Max and Layla broke apart as Kitty's voice entered the kitchen. "Oh, sorry," she said, flashing an apologetic look, "but I just tasted one of these and they are delicious." She held up a chocolate muffin.

Layla smiled as she dropped her arms from Max's neck. "I know. Presley Hays is opening up a bakery in the old laundromat, and she asked if she could place them out to drum up business."

"She'd definitely doing that. The people love them. But not as much as your burgers," she added hastily in Max's direction.

He grunted in response and Kitty continued, "Anyway, I was thinking you should contract with her. Get her to supply muffins for the bed and breakfast in the morning. I think it would be a big hit."

Layla hadn't considered that before, but Kitty had a point. If everything Presley brought in was as good as the muffin she had, then her customers would be bound to love them as well. "That is a great idea, Kitty. I'll get a contract going with her as soon as she's open."

"Just doing my duty as your best friend. Now, I'm

going to finish this muffin and then go see that adorable niece of yours."

Layla smiled as Kitty scurried out the kitchen door. Then she turned to Max and smiled up at him. "What do you say, partner? Do you want to go meet that adorable baby too?"

"I've already met her," he said with a smile, "and I'll promise I'll hold her some more, but I've got something else in mind. Think we can sneak out of here for a few minutes?"

She glanced back at his father who waved them off with his hand. "Go. I've got this covered for a few minutes, and I know who to call if I need help."

"Okay, then I'm all yours." She placed her hand in his, and Max led her out the back door.

A gasp escaped her lips as she spied the rose petals leading to the small gazebo that resided behind the bed and breakfast. "When did you have time to do this?"

"I may have had a little help," Max said with a smile. When they reached the gazebo, he leaned down and fiddled with something. She realized it was an extension cord when lights illuminated the gazebo.

"Oh, Max, this is beautiful."

"It is nowhere near as beautiful as you, but I'm hoping it will do for the perfect setting." He took her hand and held it to his heart. "Layla Montgomery, I have loved you since high school, but I was always too afraid to tell you. I'm not letting you get away this time."

As he dropped to his knee, Layla's heart thudded in her chest. She'd been proposed to - and accepted - twice before, but neither of them had felt like this. Perhaps the third time really was the charm for her.

He pulled a ring box from his pocket and flipped open the lid. "Will you make a happy man and be my wife?"

Layla nodded and held out her finger. "Yes," she whispered. She had thought she was sure with Jed. She had realized she wasn't with Randall, but as Max slid the ring on her finger, she knew without a doubt that he was the man she was destined to marry.

The End!

Not ready to see Max and Layla's story end? Want to know more about Presley? You can see them again in, When Love Returns, the next book in the Star Lake series.

16

AUTHOR'S NOTE

FIRST OFF, LET ME SAY HOW GLAD I AM THAT YOU READ this book.

I always loved The Gilmore Girls and I wanted to bring that small-town quirkiness to my book. I had always planned a story for Layla and Max and when I joined the Sweet Kisses boxed set, it became the perfect time to write it.

I hope you enjoyed this story. If you did, would you do me a favor? Please leave a review. It really helps. It doesn't have to be long - just a few words to help other readers know what they're getting.

I'd love to hear from you, not only about this story, but about the characters or stories you'd like read in the future.

I'm always looking for new ideas and if I use one of your characters or stories, I'll send you a free ebook and paperback of the book with a special dedication. Write to me at loranahoopes@gmail.com. And if you'd like to see what's coming next, be sure to stop by authorloranahoopes.com

I also have a weekly newsletter that contains many wonderful things like pictures of my adorable children, chances to win awesome prizes, new releases and sales I might be holding, great books from other authors, and anything else that strikes my fancy and that I think you would enjoy. I'll even send you the first chapter of my newest (maybe not even released yet) book if you'd like to sign up.

Even better, I solemnly swear to only send out one newsletter a week (usually on Tuesday unless life gets in the way which with three kids it usually does). I will not spam you, sell your email address to solicitors or anyone else, or any of those other terrible things.

This series will be continued, but for now, would you like to meet some characters for a new series.

PRAYERS AND BLESSINGS,
        Lorana

🌿 17 🌿
NOT READY TO SAY GOODBYE
YET?

WHEN LOVE RETURNS WAS THE ORIGINAL FIRST BOOK IN the Star Lake series. It is now the second book, but if you loved these characters, you will love them again in When Love Returns

When Love Returns

A SINGLE FATHER FORCED TO RETURN HOME

    The girl who's loved him since high school

    When the ex returns....

    Read on for a taste of When Love Returns....

WHEN LOVE RETURNS PREVIEW

There it was. The one stoplight Brandon thought he'd never see again, still blinking its irregular red pattern that no one ever paid attention to. As most of the shops were centrally located, few people drove in town. Their cars were used for driving to neighboring cities when what they wanted wasn't available in town. There was no real need for the stop light, but the people had decided the town needed at least one stoplight to be called a proper town, and so it had been erected.

There had been a huge ceremony the day it was christened; the whole town had shown up. The mayor had been forced to stand on a ladder to cut the red ribbon as someone had placed it too high. Once he was up the ladder, another member of the city board handed him a giant pair of silver scissors. Then it became a balancing act as the mayor tried to open the giant scissors without losing his balance – that had been comical – and the town had watched in awe as the stoplight blinked, blinked, long pause, blinked, blinked.

The awe had faded quickly, and a squabble had broken out among the adults about the brand new broken light. The whole affair had been rather disappointing to a sixteen-year-old, who had been looking forward to getting his driver's license. That day was the nail in the coffin that solidified Brandon's idea of leaving the tiny backwards town and returning to normalcy.

Then he had met Presley, and his life changed.

"Are we there yet, Daddy?"

Brandon glanced in the rearview mirror at his daughter, Joy, strapped in her car seat. Her dark curls came from him, but her blue-grey eyes were her mother's. Joy was the one good thing that came out of this town.

"Almost, Bug."

She resumed her stare out the window as they continued down Main Street. The Diner still sat on the corner, probably still run by Max, the same uninspired owner who wore a ball cap and plaid flannel shirt to work every day. His choice of attire left a lot to be desired, but he was a good cook. To this day, Brandon was not sure he'd had a better burger.

Next to the diner was the small Post Office. Brandon had never spent much time there growing up, but he knew the man who worked there, Ned. An odd man to say the least – always trying out new ideas that never seemed to work. One year, he had tried raising chickens to supply eggs for the general store, but he had become attached to one of the chickens, naming her Stella and carrying her from place to place in a little bag like wealthy old women do with tiny dogs. The chicken had escaped the bag one day in the middle of The Diner and wreaked havoc, incensing Max. Stella disappeared after that, and Brandon was fairly certain she ended up on Max's menu, but he could never prove it.

The general store appeared next. It carried groceries and a small selection of clothing and household goods. Brandon had been shocked by the meager selection when he first arrived, but the town wore on him and had a way of making him forget the outside world moving on around it. By the time he graduated high school, Brandon had been accustomed to the small offerings until he arrived in Dallas and felt like a total hick, at least three years behind the times.

"Daddy, look, cupcakes. Can we get one?"

Twisting in the black leather seat, Brandon followed her finger pointing out the opposite window. There had been no cupcake shop four years ago, but there was indeed a shop there now, where the laundromat had been, sporting a colorful cupcake sign and logo on the window. Sweet Treats. Not a highly original name, but neither were most of the stores in town.

"We'll come back by later." Brandon was curious about the owner. Who would choose to put up a new shop in this sleepy little town?

Her bottom lip turned out in an adorable pout, but she didn't continue to fight him. For her, this trip was like a vacation to a new and unusual place. The two rarely ventured from Dallas, mainly because Brandon's work kept him too busy for vacations. For him, it was a return to a past he had hoped to forget. Too much pain and too much sadness resided in this little town.

Brandon made a right down Cooper Street, the road that led to his parent's house. Though it had been years since he had been back, he could drive the route blindfolded, partly because it was a simple route, and partly because he walked it so many times as a teenager.

The two-story yellow house looked exactly as he remembered it, though the paint was chipping in a few more places and faded in others. The gravel of the driveway crunched under the tires as he pulled in. Brandon parked the car and took a deep breath.

"Let me out Daddy," Joy called from the back seat.

Sighing, he opened her door and then reached in to

unbuckle her. Though five, she was still too small to qualify for a booster seat, and Brandon felt safer having her in the bigger car seat anyway. No one ever told him that when he became a parent, he would have crazy nightmares about all the ways he could lose his daughter. The car accident was always the worst.

Joy scurried out of the car, her faded pink bunny clutched in one petite hand. On the day she was born, Brandon's mother had given her a soft pink cuddle bunny. Joy latched onto it, sleeping with it every night. When she began crawling, she would often pick up the bunny in her mouth, dragging it across the floors. Even after she began walking, the bunny would go outside with her to play in the dirt or be flung around the room. The bunny had seen better days, but she refused to part with it for any longer than an occasional trip in the washing machine, and of course, no one sold this bunny any longer. Brandon had scoured the internet one day looking for a replacement, but come up empty. He dreaded the day it fell apart, and he couldn't replace it.

As Joy scrambled up the wooden porch, Brandon popped the trunk and grabbed the two suitcases he packed the night before. His hope was that they'd only be here a week, but he had no guarantee and therefore packed for at least two.

Joy was banging on the door when Brandon reached her side. She hadn't been around his parents much, as

Brandon had moved to Dallas shortly after Joy's first birthday, but they had visited a few times. Joy always clung to them when they did as if she knew the time wouldn't be for very long. Now, she had created this idea in her head of what they would be like while she was here and regaled Brandon with it the last few days. He hoped she wouldn't be disappointed but was afraid she might. His mother probably wouldn't be able to spend much time with her as she would be taking care of his father, at least when he got released from the hospital.

Brandon's mother opened the door and broke into a smile. She looked older than he remembered. More lines crossed her face and more grey streaks colored her hair, but her eyes still twinkled the way they always had.

"Joy." She bent down with her arms out.

"Nana." Joy ran into her arms, squeezing the woman tightly about the neck. "You smell like cookies."

A smile played across Brandon's lips. His mother always smelled of vanilla and sugar, and while she had often had a plate of cookies waiting for him when he arrived home from school, she hadn't every day, and he wondered how she still smelled of cookies on those days.

"That's because I have some in the kitchen." She tapped the end of Joy's nose, earning a giggle. "Now, come in, and let's get you settled."

"Then can we have cookies?" Joy bounced up and

down, sending the lights in her pink sneakers into over-drive. His mother nodded, smiling at her enthusiasm.

Brandon pulled the two suitcases into the homey entrance and shut the door behind him.

The house hadn't changed a bit. A wooden coatrack still sat just to the right of the front door, holding his father's derby cap and a few coats, and the sign, announcing "As for me and my house, we will serve the Lord," still hung prominently on the wall. Brandon shed his coat, adding it to the rack and then removed Joy's as well.

"Let me show you to your room." His mother grabbed Joy's free hand and led her down the beige carpeted hall-way. Pictures of Brandon and his sister, Anna, lined the walls. His mother never let an opportunity to take a picture go by, and Brandon was almost certain she bought every school picture they ever had so she could display them all on the walls. He had tried to remove one once and replace it with something else, but she noticed right away and forced him to rehang the picture.

His mother opened the door to the guest room. She had obviously added some decorations for a younger child to enjoy. The daybed had been covered with a flowery pink and purple bedspread, and a blonde doll sat propped on top. An old dollhouse was near the dresser along with a faded toy box filled with toys.

"This is all for me?" Joy's eyes were wide as she looked up at Brandon's mother.

The lines around his mother's eyes grew more visible as she smiled. "Yep, all for you. A girl needs proper toys."

"Especially in this town," he said under his breath. Not quietly enough though as his mother shot a look full of daggers his direction. How quickly she could change from sugar to fire. Brandon held his hand up in silent apology.

"Where is Daddy staying?"

"Right across the hall." His mother opened the door to Brandon's old room which looked very much like it had in high school. His football awards still lined the shelf, though a fine layer of dust coated them now, and the tattered posters of his favorite bands covered the walls.

"Didn't feel like updating this one?" he asked.

His mother shrugged. "Maybe I would have if you came around more often."

Brandon wanted to reply, but he didn't want to start a fight, so he bit his tongue and carried the suitcase inside. After dropping off Joy's suitcase as well, they followed his mother back towards the open living room and into the country-themed kitchen. Brandon hated the flowered wallpaper trim that circled the kitchen, but his mother hung it herself and had always loved it.

A plate of chocolate chip cookies sat in the middle of the scratched kitchen table. The usual wild flower display had been pushed to the side. Joy turned eager eyes on Brandon, the unasked question evident.

"You may have one." He held up a finger. "I don't want you to spoil your dinner."

She climbed up in a chair and snatched a cookie off the top of the pile, shoving most of it in her mouth.

Brandon shook his head. "You could chew more slowly."

Her ravenous munching changed to a thoughtful chewing, and he joined her at the table, plucking a cookie for himself off the pile.

"How is Dad?" Brandon asked before taking a bite. His father was the whole reason he was here. He was in the hospital after falling off a ladder and fracturing his skull. Though Brandon's mother claimed he hadn't needed to come, he couldn't very well stay in Dallas if there was a chance this was life threatening, and brain bleeds often were.

Plus, he figured his mother might need some help with his father when he got released. He would probably not be as active as he was before the accident. However, Brandon was in the middle of a big presentation, one that could set him up for life with an even bigger company, so he had left strict instructions with his assistant to keep him in the loop.

A flicker of doubt erased his mother's twinkling eyes for a moment before she recovered. "He is doing better today. The nurses say he only had a few instances of confusion yesterday, but they want to run another CT tomorrow."

"Any idea on when he'll be released?" Brandon took a bite of the cookie, enjoying the warm chocolate goodness. He had missed his mom's cooking.

"Probably another few days, but it depends on what the scan shows. He has a pretty big brain bleed."

"Your brain can bleed?" Joy's head popped up, her eyes as wide as saucers.

His mother shot an apologetic look and without saying it, the two agreed to finish the discussion later when little ears were not present.

"Don't worry." Brandon patted her arm. "The brain is amazing and can heal itself. When does Anna get in?" Anna, his younger sister, was away at college studying to become a nurse.

"She has finals this week, so she's coming as soon as she finishes the last one. Oh, and guess who else is back in town?"

Brandon raised an eyebrow at her; he had never been a fan of the guessing game.

"Presley Hays."

Presley Hays. The name knocked the wind out of him like a sucker punch. He hadn't thought of her in years. In high school, Presley had been his best friend – the one person who had made this town bearable – but for some reason they had grown apart when Morgan entered the picture, and then one day Presley had come over to tell him she was going to France to attend Le Cordon Bleu.

"The cupcake shop?" Brandon said the words for himself, but his mother smiled and nodded.

"Who's Presley?" Joy looked from Brandon to his mother.

"Just an old friend," Brandon said. *Just an old friend.*

Continue reading When Love Returns

❧ 19 ❧
A FREE STORY FOR YOU

Enjoyed this story? Not ready to quit reading yet? If you sign up for my newsletter, you will receive The Billionaire's Impromptu Bet right away as my thank you gift for choosing to hang out with me.

The Billionaire's Impromptu Bet

A SWAT officer. A bored billionaire heiress. A bet that could change everything….

Read on for a taste of The Billionaire's Impromptu Bet….

❧ 20 ❧

THE BILLIONAIRE'S IMPROMPTU
BET PREVIEW

Brie Carter fell back spread eagle on her queen-sized canopy bed sending her blond hair fanning out behind her. With a large sigh, she uttered, "I'm bored."

"How can you be bored? You have like millions of dollars." Her friend, Ariel, plopped down in a seated position on the bed beside her and flicked her raven hair off her shoulder. "You want to go shopping? I hear Tiffany's is having a special right now."

Brie rolled her eyes. Shopping? Where was the excitement in that? With her three platinum cards, she could go shopping whenever she wanted. "No, I'm bored with shopping too. I have everything. I want to do something exciting. Something we don't normally do."

Brie enjoyed being rich. She loved the unlimited credit

cards at her disposal, the constant apparel of new clothes, and of course the penthouse apartment her father paid for, but lately, she longed for something more fulfilling.

Ariel's hazel eyes widened. "I know. There's a new bar down on Franklin Street. Why don't we go play a little game?"

Brie sat up, intrigued at the secrecy and the twinkle in Ariel's eyes. "What kind of game?"

"A betting game. You let me pick out any man in the place. Then you try to get him to propose to you."

Brie wrinkled her nose. "But I don't want to get married." She loved her freedom and didn't want to share her penthouse with anyone, especially some man.

"You don't marry him, silly. You just get him to propose."

Brie bit her lip as she thought. It had been awhile since her last relationship and having a man dote on her for a month might be interesting, but.... "I don't know. It doesn't seem very nice."

"How about I sweeten the pot? If you win, I'll set you up on a date with my brother."

Brie cocked her head. Was she serious? The only thing Brie couldn't seem to buy in the world was the affection of Ariel's very handsome, very wealthy, brother. He was a movie star, just the kind of person Brie could consider marrying in the future. She'd had a crush on him as long as she and Ariel had been friends, but he'd always seen her as just that, his little sister's friend. "I thought you didn't want me dating your brother."

"I don't." Ariel shrugged. "But he's between girl-friends right now, and I know you've wanted it for ages. If you win this bet, I'll set you up. I can't guarantee any more than one date though. The rest will be up to you."

Brie wasn't worried about that. Charm she possessed in abundance. She simply needed some alone time with him, and she was certain she'd be able to convince him they were meant to be together. "All right. You've got a deal."

Ariel smiled. "Perfect. Let's get you changed then and see who the lucky man will be.

A tiny tug pulled on Brie's heart that this still wasn't right, but she dismissed it. This was simply a means to an end, and he'd never have to know.

JESSE CALHOUN RELAXED AS THE RHYTHMIC THUDDING OF the speed bag reached his ears. Though he loved his job, it was stressful being the SWAT sniper. He hated having to take human lives and today had been especially rough. The team had been called out to a drug bust, and Jesse was forced to return fire at three hostiles. He didn't care that they fired at his team and himself first. Taking a life was always hard, and every one of them haunted his dreams.

"You gonna bust that one too?" His co-worker Brendan

appeared by his side. Brendan was the opposite of Jesse in nearly every way. Where Jesse's hair was a dark copper, Brendan's was nearly black. Jesse sported paler skin and a dusting of freckles across his nose, but Brendan's skin was naturally dark and freckle free.

Jesse flashed a crooked grin, but kept his eyes on the small, swinging black bag. The speed bag was his way to release, but a few times he had started hitting while still too keyed up and he had ruptured the bag. Okay, five times, but who was counting really? Besides, it was a better way to calm his nerves than other things he could choose. Drinking, fights, gambling, women.

"Nah, I think this one will last a little longer." His shoulders began to burn, and he gave the bag another few punches for good measure before dropping his arms and letting it swing to a stop. "See? It lives to be hit at least another day." Every once in a while, Jesse missed training the way he used to. Before he joined the force, he had been an amateur boxer, on his way to being a pro, but a shoulder injury had delayed his training and forced him to consider something else. It had eventually healed, but by then he had lost his edge.

"Hey, why don't you come drink with us?" Brendan clapped a hand on Jesse's shoulder as they headed into the locker room.

"You know I don't drink." Jesse often felt like the outsider of the team. While half of the six-man team was married, the other half found solace in empty bottles and meaningless relationships. Jesse understood that - their job was such that they never knew if they would come home night after night - but he still couldn't partake.

Brendan opened his locker and pulled out a clean shirt. He peeled off his current one and added deodorant before tugging on the new one. "You don't have to drink. Look, I won't drink either. Just come and hang out with us. You have no one waiting for you at home."

That wasn't entirely true. Jesse had Bugsy, his Boston Terrier, but he understood Brendan's point. Most days, Jesse went home, fed Bugsy, made dinner, and fell asleep watching TV on the couch. It wasn't much of a life. "All right, I'll go, but I'm not drinking."

Brendan's lips pulled back to reveal his perfectly white teeth. He bragged about them, but Jesse knew they were veneers. "That's the spirit. Hurry up and change. We don't want to leave the rest of the team waiting."

"Is everyone coming?" Jesse pulled out his shower necessities. Brendan might feel comfortable going out with just a new application of deodorant, but Jesse needed to wash more than just dirt and sweat off. He needed to wash the sound of the bullets and the sight of lifeless bodies from his mind.

"Yeah, Pat's wife is pregnant again and demanding some crazy food concoctions. Pat agreed to pick them up if she let him have an hour. Cam and Jared's wives are having a girls' night, so the whole gang can be together. It will be nice to hang out when we aren't worried about being shot at."

"Fine. Give me ten minutes. Unlike you, I like to clean up before I go out."

Brendan smirked. "I've never had any complaints. Besides, do you know how long it takes me to get my hair like this?"

Jesse shook his head as he walked into the shower, but he knew it was true. Brendan had rugged good looks and muscles to match. He rarely had a hard time finding a woman. Jesse on the other hand hadn't dated anyone in the last few months. It wasn't that he hadn't been looking, but he was quieter than his teammates. And he wasn't looking for right now. He was looking for forever. He just hadn't found it yet.

Click here to continue reading The Billionaire's Impromptu Bet.

THE STORY DOESN'T END!

You've met a few people and fallen in love….

I bet you're wondering how you can meet everyone else.

Star Lake Series:

Sealed with a Kiss: Meet the quirky cast of Star Lake and find out if Max and Layla will ever find love.

When Love Returns: Return to Star Lake to hear Presley's story and find out if she gets the second chance with her first love.

Once Upon a Star: Continue the journey when aspiring actress Audrey returns home with a baby. Will Blake finally get the nerve to share his feelings with her?

Love Conquers All: Meet Lanie Perkins Hall who never imagined being divorced at thirty or falling for an old friend, but will his secrets keep them apart?

The Star Lake Collection: Get the latter three stories in one place. Series will include book 1 when it releases around November 2020.

The Heartbeats Series:

Where It All Began: Sandra Baker finds forgiveness and healing even after making a horrible choice.

The Power of Prayer: Will Callie Green find true love or be defined by her mistake?

When Hearts Collide: When Amanda Adams goes to college, she finds a world she was not ready for. But will she also find true love?

A Past Forgiven: Jess Peterson has lived a life of abuse and lost her self worth, but when she finds herself pregnant, will she find new hope?

The Heartbeats Collection: Grab all four Heartbeats novels in one collection

Sweet Billionaires Series:

The Billionaire's Impromptu Bet: Can a spoiled rich girl change when a bet turns to love?

The Billionaire's Secret: Can a playboy settle down when he finds out he has a daughter who needs him?

A Brush with a Billionaire: What happens when a stuck up actor lands in a small town and needs help from a female mechanic?

The Billionaire's Christmas Miracle: A twist on a Cinderella story when a billionaire meets a woman who doesn't belong at the ball.

The Billionaire's Cowboy Groom: Will one night six years ago keep Carrie from finding true love?

The Cowboy Billionaire: Coming Soon!

The Billionaire's Bliss: This collection contains The Billionaire's Secret, The Billionaire's Christmas Miracle, and The Billionaire's Cowboy Groom

The Lawkeeper Series:

Lawfully Matched: When the man she agreed to marry turns out to have a dark past, will Kate have to return home or will she find love with her rescuer in this historical fiction?

Lawfully Justified: Can a bounty hunter and a widow find love together in this historical fiction?

The Scarlet Wedding: William and Emma are planning their wedding, but an outbreak and a return from his past force them to change their plans. Is a happily ever after still in their future in this historical fiction?

Lawfully Redeemed: What happens when a K9 cop falls for the brother of her suspect? Contemporary romance.

The Lawkeeper Collection: Get all four books in one collection

The Are You Listening Series:

The Still Small Voice: Will Jordan listen to God's prompting in this speculative fiction?

A Spark in the Darkness Will Jordan be able to help Raven before the rapture occurs?

Blushing Brides Series:

The Cowboy's Reality Bride: He's agreed to be the bachelor on a reality dating show, but what happens when he falls for a woman who's not one of the contestants?

The Reality Bride's Baby: Laney wants nothing more than a baby, but when she starts feeling dizzy is it pregnancy or something more serious?

The Producer's Unlikely Bride: What happens when a producer and an author agree to a fake relationship?

Ava's Blessing in Disguise: Five years after marriage, Ava faces a mysterious illness that threatens to ruin her career. Will she find out what it is?

The Soldier's Steadfast Bride: coming soon

The Men of Fire Beach

Fire Games: Cassidy returns home from Who Wants to Marry a Cowboy to find obsessive letters from a fan. The cop assigned to help her wants to get back to his case, but what she sees at a fire may just be the key he's looking for.

Lost Memories and New Beginnings: A doctor, a patient with no memory, the men out to get her. Can he keep her safe when he doesn't know who he's looking for?

When Questions Abound: A Companion story to Lost Memories. Told from Detective Graves' point of view.

Never Forget the Past: Fireman Bubba must confront his past in order to clear his name and save lives.

Love on the Run: Graham is forced into lockdown

with one of his employees. Will he be able to save her from her ex and will she steal his heart?

Secrets and Suspense: Cara Hunter is hiding something about her military past. When she's suspected of murder, will she be able to convince Cole she's the victim?

The Men of Fire Beach Collection: Books 1-3

Texas Tornadoes

Defending My Heart: Forced to confront his past, Emmitt finds news that will change his life.

Run With My Heart: Sentenced to community service, Tucker finds himself falling for the manager.

Love on the Line: Blaine has hired Kenzi to redo his cabin, but what happens when she finds his darkest secret?

Touchdown on Love: When Mason's injury throws him together with ex-girlfriend, will sparks fly again?

Second Chance Reception: Jefferson is hiding something. When he falls for the team cook, will he let her in?

Small Town Short Stories

Small Town Dreams

Small Town Second Chances

Small Town Rivals

Small Town Life

Life in a Small Town: All four stories in one collection

Stand Alones:

Love Renewed: This books is part of the multi author second chance series. When fate reunites high school sweethearts separated by life's choices, can they find a second chance at love at a snowy lodge amid a little mystery?

Her children's early reader chapter book series:
    The Wishing Stone #1: Dangerous Dinosaur
    The Wishing Stone #2: Dragon Dilemma
    The Wishing Stone #3: Mesmerizing Mermaids
    The Wishing Stone #4: Pyramid Puzzle
    The Wishing Stone Inspirations 1: Mary's Miracle
    To see a list of all her books

authorloranahoopes.com
loranahoopes@gmail.com

DISCUSSION QUESTIONS

1. What was your favorite scene in the book? What made it your favorite?

2. Did you have a favorite line in the book? What do you think made it so memorable?

3. Who was your favorite character in the book and why?

4. What do you think would be the hardest part about seeing an old flame?

5. What did you learn about God from reading this book?

6. How can you use that knowledge in your life from now on?

7. What do you think would make the story even better?

ABOUT THE AUTHOR

Lorana Hoopes is an inspirational author originally from Texas but now living in the PNW with her husband and three children. When not writing, she can be seen kick-boxing at the gym, singing, or acting on stage. One day, she hopes to retire from teaching and write full time.

www.ingramcontent.com/pod-product-compliance
Lightning Source LLC
Chambersburg PA
CBHW022032170626
46808CB00003B/1152